FROZ

It was Dain Ransome's skill as a lecturer
on a riveting subject that had fired Kerin
with the idea of joining an expedition to
the Antarctic, not the man himself—he
had struck her as a particularly unpleasant mixture of arrogance and icy coldness. So she was considerably taken aback
to discover that he was the leader of the
expedition ...

Books you will enjoy
by DAPHNE CLAIR

THE LOVING TRAP

The dislike that had at first sprung up between Kyla Vernon and Marc Nathan soon turned into love, and when he asked her to marry him she accepted—although with secret misgivings. Would she be able to overcome her reluctance to commit herself—or was the marriage doomed from the very beginning?

A WILDER SHORE

'Next time it's going to be me,' Shard Cortland told Elise uncompromisingly after her first husband Peter died—and perhaps she ought to have married Shard in the first place. So she married Shard at last. In the circumstances, they should both have been blissfully happy—so just what was going wrong with their marriage?

DARLING DECEIVER

At seventeen, Carissa had been a silly, romantic teenager, in love with a dream called Cade Fernand—which was why she had behaved the way she had on the one occasion they had met. Now, eight years later, they had met again, and she had no reason to suppose Cade remembered anything about her. But he still remembered—and still despised her. And Carissa realised, hopelessly, that her feelings for Cade had not changed either ...

SOMETHING LESS THAN LOVE

Just what had gone wrong with Vanessa's marriage? True, her husband Thad had been badly injured in a car crash soon after the wedding, but he was recovering now. It wasn't that—it was his curious, bitter, suspicious attitude towards her. What was she supposed to have *done*?

FROZEN HEART

BY

DAPHNE CLAIR

MILLS & BOON LIMITED
15–16 BROOK'S MEWS
LONDON W1A 1DR

First published 1980
Australian copyright 1980
Philippine copyright 1980
This edition 1980

© Daphne Clair 1980

ISBN 0 263 73427 7

Set in Linotype Plantin 10 on 10½ pt.

Made and printed in Great Britain by
Richard Clay (The Chaucer Press), Ltd., Bungay, Suffolk

CHAPTER ONE

KERIN threw the last of her sandwich into the smooth-flowing water of the Avon, and watched while a gaggle of greedy ducks fought over it with a flurry of wings and indignant argument. The willows that were supposed to be descendants of slips brought to New Zealand from the island of St Helena when Napoleon was exiled there trailed into the water from the neatly mown riverside, and trim flowerbeds between spreading trees splashed the park with colour.

Typically Christchurch, she thought, suddenly a little impatient with the beautiful order of it all. She was actually very fond of the city and had spent most of her life here, in this most 'English' corner of New Zealand. The early settlers had chosen a piece of the flat Canterbury Plains (even those named for a place in their homeland!) and had transformed the alien landscape into a modest copy of an English town, with well-planned streets, solid 'gothic' buildings of grey stone, and carefully tended parks lining the banks of the river they had called after the one that belonged to Shakespeare's town.

They had bequeathed to their descendants a city of rare grace and charm, of which those descendants were for the most part quietly proud—and to Kerin Paige, at least, a modicum of that spirit of adventure which had led the early wanderers to pack up families and possessions and emigrate to an unknown future in a small group of islands at the other side of the earth.

She was suffering now, she recognised, from a mild attack of a recurrent malady—wanderlust, or 'itchy feet'.

'Dear, oh, dear!' she murmured to herself, with a rueful smile, and leaned back against the bark of the willow be-

5

hind her, stretching long legs out on the grass and crossing a slim pair of ankles.

No. It wouldn't do at all. She had a very good job on the staff of the outdoor magazine *Adventure*, a comfortable flat in the city shared with a friend from her schooldays, and perhaps most important, a man in her life who was gradually becoming rather special to her.

No, she told herself again. Time you settled down, my girl. Time, perhaps, to think about marriage. Opportunity wasn't lacking. Her dark shoulder-length hair framed an oval face with a straight nose, warm hazel eyes and a beautifully feminine mouth, and she had no special vices. She was aware that her figure curved in the right places, too, and that some of her female friends frankly envied her looks. She never lacked for male attention—in fact, she noticed with slight amusement, as her gaze wandered idly about the landscape, she was attracting some now.

The man was leaning on the parapet of a nearby bridge, quite near enough for her to read the look of lazy appreciation on his face as he watched her.

She appraised him with swift impersonality before moving her own gaze away. She didn't want him to think she was looking for a pick-up.

Quite attractive, she decided, in a slightly chilly way. He was fair-haired, light-eyed—blue or grey, it was difficult to tell. Regular features, almost classic, except that a certain breadth about the cheekbones and chin added unexpected strength to the face, an impression of determination, even power, that was reinforced as he suddenly straightened and she saw he must be quite tall, perhaps a bit more than six feet. His hands gripped at the wooden railing of the bridge for a few moments, and she saw the strength in them, too, before he moved them.

He was coming her way, and she got quickly to her feet and turned, walking rapidly away. It was time she was moving on anyway. Having lunch by the river had been pleasant, but she had to be at the Canterbury Club by two o'clock.

It was probably this assignment, she thought, pursuing her previous line of thinking, that had caused her faint restlessness. The speaker she was to listen to was Dain Ransome, just back from the Antarctic, and, according to the background information she had looked up on him, a man with a large wanderlust of his own. With a background in geology, he was respected as a scientist and had written several dozen papers of a learned specialist nature, and a book on volcanoes which she gathered incorporated a lot of first-hand knowledge, and some pretty spectacular photographic close-ups of volcanic activity which he had taken himself.

He had first gone to Antarctica at the age of twenty-five —her own age now, Kerin reflected—and it must have hooked him, because since then he had spent several seasons there, and at thirty-four he was recognised as one of the few who could be said to know the region fairly well.

Well, he should be interesting, and she expected to be able to write up his talk into a feature for the magazine with little trouble, perhaps with the help of a short interview with him afterwards. Roger Harris, her boss and the man in her life, had tried to organise an exclusive interview, but Ransome was hard to pin down, apparently very much in demand and, so he said, short of time.

He also, Roger had indicated ruefully, seemed to have little respect for magazines such as *Adventure*.

'He said,' Roger told her, 'something about "armchair adventurers who get their kicks from vicarious experience served up secondhand and warmed over by hack writers with heart conditions". Which he implied they wouldn't have if they spent time doing things instead of writing about people who *do* do them.'

'Did he indeed!' Kerin said indignantly. 'He sounds like an arrogant beast. He's probably never even read the magazine!'

'He's certainly never met a journalist like you,' said Roger, smiling slyly. 'I thought you might like to cut along to this lecture of his that we've been rather grudgingly allowed to send a reporter to. He said, "I'll be speaking at the Canterbury Club, Wednesday, two o'clock. Send a reporter if you like." So, darling, I'm sending you.'

She eyed his bland smile with faint suspicion, and asked, 'Why me?'

Roger laughed. 'Because you're a knock-out, and I'd like to see his face—though unfortunately I can't come along and do so—when he sees what sort of "hack writer with a heart condition" we send. And because I hope like most men he's susceptible enough to let you charm him into giving you a short interview, at least, after the lecture. Turn it on, will you, honey, and try to thaw him a bit?'

'I know what you mean,' she told him. 'But I don't think I approve. I'm a journalist, not a—a——'

'Don't say it!' he grinned. 'Yes, I know you're a feminist, darling, and no doubt it's all very sexist and all that. Let's just say you've more charm than Willie Webster, and leave it at that—please?'

She laughed and left it. Willie Webster would have confirmed all the Ransome man's worst suspicions—overweight, balding and obviously out of condition, he was a surprisingly good interviewer who spent a lot of time at airports and hotel bars cornering his subjects. When he was much younger he had been known to accompany them to unlikely spots such as bush camps deep in the heart of Fiordland where deerstalkers plied their trade, or remote outlying islands only accessible by helicopter. Willie declared himself now past all that and cheerfully blamed his deterioration on drink and loose living, which, he declared with a booming laugh, he had no intention of giving up.

'Do I take a camera?' she asked Roger.

'No. He said no photos. If we want one we can probably get a print from the Antarctic Division of the Department of Scientific and Industrial Research.' He paused. 'Anyway, I can get someone else on to that. You get down there Wednesday and get the story for me.'

Well, she would get the story. She hoped he *was* an interesting speaker, not one of those who rambled on inter-

minably in scientific jargon that bored the listeners to tears,
when what they wanted was a spark of imagination and
enthusiasm that would bring the place, the excitement of
discovery and adventure alive for them. If he turned out
to be one of *those* it would be up to her to liven up the story
with some carefully researched embellishments of her own
about the man and his subject.

She had left the park and stopped at a traffic light, watching idly as a phalanx of young cyclists from the very
'English public school' of Christ's College passed by. The
youngsters were not the only cyclists, though. The city's
wide, flat streets were ideal for that mode of transport,
which had always been popular and was enjoying a resur-
gence due to the fuel crisis.

Someone came to stand beside her, and she cast a swift
glance at a tall figure, to find the man from the bridge regarding her with a quizzical look from eyes that she could
see now were blue—a rather cool blue, but they were taking
a warm interest in her.

She looked away and the light changed, but he was still
beside her as she reached the other side of the road. He
didn't speak, but kept pace with her, and she began to feel
a faint warmth of annoyance in her cheeks. When she
looked at him again he was staring straight ahead, and she
wondered if it was just coincidence after all.

But when she turned into the building she had been
making for and entered the lift in the lobby, he walked in
beside her and said, 'Which floor?' his hand poised over
the buttons.

'Second,' she said, after a slight hesitation.

The doors had closed, but he didn't press the button
straight away. He glanced rather teasingly over her trim
figure in the light wool, belted coat and commented, 'You're
a brisk walker. I'd have thought two flights of stairs would
be nothing for you.'

'Why don't *you* go—climb the stairs?' she asked him
sweetly, and repeated firmly, '*Second* floor, please.'

He laughed a little, which took the slightly cold look

from his face altogether, and pressed the button.

'I have my reasons,' he said, leaning against the wall, his blue eyes full of meaning. 'You know, you're what's known as a sight for sore eyes. And you don't know how sincerely I mean that.'

He didn't look sincere, he looked derisive and very slightly admiring, in an almost clinical way, like a judge at a flower show who admires the blooms but is also weighing up their flaws and assessing the precise degree of their beauty.

Kerin didn't care for it much, and as the lift came to a stop, just before the doors opened she said bluntly, 'Are you following me?'

'Of course. Where are we going?'

She stepped out of the lift into a carpeted corridor and turned on him as he followed. 'I don't know where *you're* going,' she said crisply. '*I'm* going to listen to a lecture.'

'What about?' he asked, as she made to turn away.

'Antarctic geology.'

'Sounds fascinating.'

'It does not!' she snapped. 'It sounds dead boring, and it probably will be.'

'That will depend on the speaker, surely.'

'The speaker is an arrogant, pigheaded intellectual snob,' she told him.

Just for an instant the man in front of her looked faintly startled, then his eyes narrowed and she saw he was amused. 'You know him?'

'Not exactly. I know *about* him—look, I have to go——'

Determinedly, she turned again and began walking down the corridor.

When he fell into step beside her she didn't stop, but said coldly, 'You can't come. It's a private club.'

'Will you meet me afterwards?'

'No.'

'Then I'm coming.'

'They won't let you in,' she warned him.

He laughed softly and said confidently, 'Oh, I think they will.'

Kerin looked at him briefly and realised what an air of confidence he had, as though he could do anything he wanted, once he set his mind to it—and knew it.

As they neared the open door to the room where the meeting was to be held, he said, 'You could say I'm with you.'

Tempted, she almost agreed. Usually she didn't go for fair men, but this one, apart from looking like a latter-day Viking, was having some sort of powerful effect on her usual good sense. She didn't care for casual pick-ups, but although he admitted following her and was clearly interested, he hadn't been offensive.

But she had a job to do, and besides, in a personal as well as a professional capacity, she felt she owed some loyalty to Roger. Firmly she said, 'No. Sorry,' and turning into the doorway she flashed her presscard at the man behind the small table just inside the room and found herself a seat at the back, refraining with an effort from looking round to see how the man was faring, if he had really attempted to enter.

She made herself think of Roger, of the intimate dinner they had shared only last Saturday night, of the sweet moments in his car afterwards when he kissed her and murmured that he loved her. It was the first time he had said that, in so many words, and she didn't yet feel quite ready to reciprocate, but she found him a good companion and his lovemaking was considerate and yet exciting. He had been hinting lately that he was tired of bachelorhood, and she was quite sure that before long he was going to ask her to marry him. And she already had nearly decided that she would accept. There was absolutely no point in rocking the boat of their gradually growing happiness and confidence in each other for the sake of some cheap adventure with a chance-met stranger. He wasn't the first man to attract her, and he wouldn't be the last, she supposed, but sexual attraction was capricious and unreliable. It wasn't lacking in her relationship with Roger, by any means, only it was underpinned by much more solid qualities of mutual liking and respect.

'Hello, Kerin!'

She turned to see a girl of about her own age sliding into the seat beside her. Val Lamont worked for one of the big daily papers. She was an attractive girl with bouncy red hair and a sprinkling of freckles ornamenting a creamy skin.

'Hello, Val, I didn't realise you were covering this beat now.'

'I finally managed to persuade my boss there's more to life than the women's pages and the gardening news. When I heard him lamenting that Dain Ransome wouldn't give an interview and he'd have to send someone out here to cover his talk, I threatened him with the Human Rights Act if he didn't send me! Apart from everything else, I've been half in love with the man since seeing him on television—I can't wait to meet him in person.'

Kerin laughed. 'So I've got a rival.'

'What, you too?' Val asked smilingly.

'Not exactly. I've never seen the man—even on television. But Roger wants an interview very badly. When Ransome finishes the lecture I'll be up there batting my eyelashes and exuding feminine allure for all I'm worth.' Giving Val a preview performance, she cooed, 'Oh, Mr Ransome— you're so handsome! And your lecture was *divine*! Well, something like that, anyway,' she added, in her normal tones. 'I'm supposed to be here because, quote: I have more charm than Willie Webster: unquote. Mr Ransome will get the full benefit of it—and I'll get what I want, I hope.'

Val rolled her eyes in comic dismay. 'All *I* want is Mr Ransome!' she smiled. Solemnly she put out a hand. 'May the best girl win!'

Kerin laughed and accepted the handshake. Val was fun, and a good reporter. It might be true that she had liked

Dain Ransome's looks, but like Kerin, she was here primarily to get a story. All the rest was fooling.

A few minutes later a group of people went up to the front of the room and the chairman called for silence.

Kerin hastily took out her notebook and pencil from her bag and flipped over the pages to be ready for the main speaker. It wasn't until a spattering of applause greeted the end of the chairman's introduction and Val whispered in her ear with a hint of laughter, 'There, what do you say? Isn't he a gorgeous blond beast?' that she looked up at the man who had stepped forward and stood behind the lectern, surveying the audience with a faint, confident smile on his firmly chiselled mouth.

The man from the park. The man she had snubbed. The man she had accused of following her. And—*oh, my gosh!* she thought. The man to whom she had said, 'The speaker is an arrogant, pigheaded intellectual snob.'

Dain Ransome.

What did she do now?

Of course, there was nothing she could do, except apologise later when she got the chance. He might have *told* her! The beast, she thought indignantly. Of course he hadn't been following her—he must have thought she had colossal vanity.

But he *had* been giving her interested looks, hadn't he?

Or had he? There had been that air of detachment even as he inspected her. Had he merely been thinking that *she* thought he was interested, and wondering why she should imagine he would bother with her?

He had said he was following her because it amused him to say so. He had been amused, after his first shock, when she told him her opinion of the then unknown Dain Ransome. So at least he had a sense of humour. And he *had* asked her to meet him afterwards. She wondered if he had meant that, or had it been a part of the act he had put on after she accused him of following her.

With an effort she wrenched her mind back to the present moment. Dain Ransome was speaking, and Val had her head down, making rapid notes. She must concentrate on what the man was saying.

'... and the continent contains ninety per cent of all the ice in the world,' she heard, and dutifully wrote it down, followed by '... the lowest temperatures in the world ... the strongest winds ... the hardiest animal life ... richest ocean ... at the Pole the snow is three hundred feet deep, then a solid sheet of ice; the land is hidden under seven thousand and five hundred feet of snow and ice ...'

He's a statistical speaker, Kerin thought, her pencil pausing for a moment as he went on to say that if the polar icecap melted the oceans would rise two hundred feet all around the world, and many great seaside cities would disappear. She wrote *that* down, quickly translating it to mean that New Zealand's capital, Wellington, would be swallowed up, and the Queen City, Auckland, as well as New York, Sydney ...

That might interest her readers, remote as the possibility seemed, but too many statistics would only bore them, however fascinating the facts were in themselves. *Two hundred feet*, she thought. Would Christchurch and the Plains go under, she wondered, or would the Port Hills protect the city? Probably not, she decided. The city would drown.

But now he was describing the phenomenon of the Aurora Australis, and his hands left the lectern and began weaving patterns in the air as he tried to show them the different shapes of the strange lights in the winter sky, and his voice became quiet and almost hypnotic as he told them how it felt to stand on the vast polar icecap and watch a beautiful, eerie display of moving, rainbow lights flash and shimmer, glow, fall and spread in ever-changing patterns across the empty darkness.

His voice was beautiful, she realised, deep and velvety, and as she listened tiny tingles of excitement ran up and down her spine. She closed her eyes and pictured the spectacle that he was painting with words, with that beautiful masculine voice.

Then he began to talk about the scientific aspects of the

Aurora, the theories as to its probable causes, and the methods used to record and analyse its occurrence in the Antarctic. Kerin's pencil flew again and she wrote '... possibly caused by some sort of electro-magnetic activity in the ionosphere ...' and put a question mark after that because she didn't have the faintest idea what it meant. Then she put, 'modern instruments analyse the frequency of light waves ...' If *she* didn't understand it, perhaps *some* readers with a scientific bent might nevertheless find it interesting.

Personally, she liked the sound of the all-sky camera with the spherical lens that he was describing now, which took cine-films of the Aurora for the scientists to study at leisure. Now *that* would be something to see, if one couldn't go down to the polar continent and watch the thing itself.

Pity he hadn't some film with him, she thought, but was soon lost in his description of the ice caves near Scott Base, with their rarely beautiful ice stalactites and stalagmites and what he called 'the ultimate purity of nature.'

It was an odd phrase, but when he said it she knew what he meant, because he had made her *see* it, so that when she closed her eyes again she could imagine the peace and the fantastic quiet of the ice shelf, the lamplight playing on the natural ice sculptures in the caves.

But as the lecture progressed she found it hard to wrench her eyes from the speaker even to make her necessary notes. He used his hands sparingly but with effect. They were sensitive hands, but strong, the palm broad but the fingers long and expressive. And his face as he spoke became at times intense with some very fierce, though controlled emotion. In a strange, distant way she felt it herself, reaching out from him, a pull on the senses, on the mind.

Like a lover, she thought, with a faint, appalled shock. That was how he spoke, with tenderness and admiration and a kind of eager pride, and at times, when he told them about difficulties and dangers and the men who had died in blizzards and in falls into bottomless crevasses or into water so cold that freezing to death was a greater risk than drowning, and lately in air crashes against snow-shrouded mountains, then there was also an element of tough determination there, a wary respect mixed with refusal to be cowed. His love was cruel and cold and beautiful, and the only way to respond to her call was with courage and challenge and a will to conquer.

'... Dain Ransome's love ...' she wrote on her pad, and began adding words in her mind, telling her readers of this man's savage and sensitive love for a mistress that was five million square miles of remote, ice-cold beauty ...

And then she looked up again at his face and wondered if he knew how much of himself he had revealed today to her, to all of them in that room.

She looked around at their faces and saw them looking interested, amused, some even slightly bored, and she realised that none of them, even though they were enjoying the talk, were feeling as involved as she did. None of them had seen in Dain Ransome's face the raw emotion that she saw so clearly, that she *felt* in her very being, an emotional storm of minor dimensions but tangible all the same.

Her eyes dropped to the three words on the pad, and she lifted her pencil and scrubbed them out, blackly obliterating them. One didn't reveal a man's soul wilfully to an uncaring, careless world ... That story would never be written.

When he had finished there was a very enthusiastic burst of applause, and then a few questions from the floor which he answered briefly and clearly.

Then the chairman indicated that the meeting was at an end, and Val shot up and scooted with speed and decorum to the front of the room, while Kerin was still gradually coming down to earth, and trying to formulate in her mind how she was going to approach the man.

When she did, he was talking to Val, and seemingly enjoying himself. A man interrupted them for a minute and Val got her pad and pencil poised. Kerin had put hers away as too blatant in the circumstances. She wanted to get in a graceful, rueful apology first before angling for an interview, and she rather hoped that his invitation to join him still stood, because it would make for a much more satisfactory interview, and besides, she had discovered a definite desire to get to know Ransome better.

The minute the man turned away, she edged in quickly with her shoulder half-turned to Val and touched his arm with light, firm fingers.

The fair head turned and she discovered that close up the blue eyes had a devastating effect when his smile reached them. But the smile was evidently not for her, for it faded as his brows rose. They were straight and much darker than his hair, and his lashes matched them, giving character to his eyes and making them seem, perhaps, more vivid than they were. But right now, they were rapidly cooling.

She said with sincerity, 'Thank you for a marvellous talk, Mr Ransome. I don't remember when I've been so enthralled.'

His mouth smiled then, but his eyes retained their disconcerting coolness. 'Antarctic geology isn't so boring, after all?'

'There was a good deal more than geology in it.' she answered, smiling. 'But I'm sorry about that—of course, I didn't know who you were—I hope you still would like——'

But he said curtly, 'Apology accepted.' And then he turned from her to take Val by the arm and walk her away with him to where the chairman was chatting to some other people, and she heard him say, 'Look, why don't we continue this interview in quieter surroundings, after I've said my goodbyes to this crowd?'

As he shook the chairman's hand, Val looked round to where Kerin still stood, trying to regain her poise after that calculated snub, and made a little face of surprise and apology. But she didn't try to hide the fact that she was pleased with herself.

Kerin pulled herself together and gave a rueful shrug and a smile back, with a tiny thumbs-up sign. *May the best girl win*, they had said, jokingly. And there was no doubt about it, Val had won hands down.

Well, she deserved it, and Kerin didn't grudge her friend the small victory. She just wished *she* didn't feel quite so much the loser.

CHAPTER TWO

'THE man's a conceited, pompous egotist!' she told Roger later.

'Wasn't the talk any good?' the editor asked mildly.

'Oh, the *talk* was all right!' she admitted angrily, throwing herself into a chair and shucking off her shoes. 'Well, actually——' she added reluctantly, '—actually, the talk was fantastic.'

Roger leaned his lanky frame against his desk, folded arms clad in immaculate coat-sleeves with just the right amount of cuff showing, and raised his dark eyebrows at her. 'Well, then?'

'I didn't get the interview,' she confessed.

Annoyance darkened his handsome face for an instant, but then he smiled at her. 'Never mind, darling, I'm sure it was a good try. We can't *make* a man talk to the press.'

'Not this member of it, anyway,' she muttered resignedly.

'Honey, if you couldn't persuade him, no one could.'

'Wrong,' she told him ruefully. 'Val Lamont did. I think she's getting an exclusive, and it'll be good, too.'

'Val Lamont?' Roger looked startled, and then to her surprise began to laugh. 'You mean Val pipped you to the post? Is *that* why you're so upset about it?'

Reluctant to tell him the whole story, she shrugged and asked, 'Isn't it enough?'

Regarding her with speculative amusement, he said teasingly, 'Your feminism doesn't go very deep, does it? Talk about female rivalry—you're furious because Ransome preferred Val to you. Never mind, darling, the man's obviously blind or mad——'

'Of course it isn't that!' she snapped. 'I'm furious because she got an interview and I didn't! And it isn't Val that I'm angry with——'

With laughter in his dark eyes, he said soothingly, 'Of course not.' He came away from the desk and scooped her up out of the chair and into his arms. 'But anger becomes you, my sweet,' he murmured. 'Kiss me.'

She didn't respond immediately to the feel of his mouth on hers, still annoyed that he had construed her fury as feminine vanity, and too strung up to suddenly change from one mood to the other. But after a moment she let his strong arms pull her closer and wound hers about his neck, trying to drown her anger and the faint but nagging sense of hurt ...

Roger's mouth lifted from hers and he smiled down at her and said, 'Blind or mad. Val Lamont can't hold a candle to you. *God*, but you're beautiful!'

He found her mouth again with eager passion, and his hands moved over her back, shaping the narrowness of her waist, then shifting again to find the curves of her breasts.

Kerin pulled away, her cheeks flushed, and fumbled for her shoes. She put them on and put up a hand to straighten her hair, smoothing it back over her ears, and dared to look at Roger.

He stood with his hands in his pockets, regarding her with a mixture of curiosity and amusement. 'You're very shy,' he said, 'for a girl who's been around as much as you have.'

She said, 'If you mean what I think you do——'

'No!' Roger said hastily. 'Sorry. I meant you've travelled a good deal, not only in this country but the East, the continent, the islands. Off the beaten track too, even in North Africa, you told me, with a mixed group of girls and young men.'

'Yes, well, it didn't include mixed bedrooms,' she said tartly. 'There are some places it's more convenient to have a mixed party. There are still countries where women on their own are regarded with suspicion—or as fair game for any passing male, unfortunately.'

'What about the stint you did crewing on that yacht round the Pacific?'

'*What* about it?' she asked, regarding him steadily.

'You said the captain was the only male on board.'

'That's right.'

'Well?'

'Well—what? Did you think I was one of his floating harem?'

'No, of course not. It's just that—well, you must admit it was a pretty funy set-up, Kerin.'

'Was it? The captain happened to be the father of one of the girls, Roger. We were all on holiday from the university and we were all good friends. Carol's father needed a crew, and he had no male hang-ups about an all-girl crew, he trusted our ability. He's a very nice man who would never have dreamed of making the mildest pass at one of his daughter's friends. And on shore he looked after us all as though we *were* his daughters. Satisfied?'

'I'm sorry, Kerin. But thank you for telling me. I suppose you think I've no right to ask you about—well, I suppose I haven't yet, but you know how I feel about you. So don't mind if I ask questions, will you?'

She looked at him frankly, saying, 'That depends on the question. And I suppose this—licence to question applies to me, too?'

He looked very slightly startled at that, and she almost laughed. Roger was a very attractive person, and she didn't suppose he had learned how to make love to a girl in his really quite expert fashion from sitting behind a desk. She didn't mind that too much, but it *had* crossed her mind that a roving eye wouldn't necessarily be stopped from wandering by the exchange of wedding vows—unless he meant them with all his heart. And so far she wasn't quite sure how much Roger's heart was involved in their affair. Sometimes she had the chilling feeling that he had been looking for someone he could bear to spend the rest of his life with, and she had just happened along at the right moment.

Not that there was anything so wrong about that—in fact, she had to admit that to a certain extent it applied to her as well. Probably they were lucky to have found each other. Maybe fate had taken a hand.

'Anyway,' she said, 'I'd better go and write up this talk.'

Roger nodded, and she wondered if he looked slightly relieved as she left the office, or if that was her imagination.

It didn't take long to turn out a competent and interesting article based on the Ransome lecture. She knew it lacked the extra spark that might have resulted if she could have interviewed the man himself, but had to be satisfied with what she could make of it.

When she went home to the flat that night there was a note from her flatmate to say she had gone out for dinner and would be late. Kerin cooked herself a light meal and tried to read a book, but pictures kept floating into her mind of a snow-covered landscape, of icebergs floating on a deep green sea, of a man with a light of passionate feeling in his face.

Eventually she took out her small portable typewriter and some fresh copy paper, and began to type ...

Val's feature article incorporating the exclusive interview she had got from Dain Ransome appeared two days later, spread over a whole page. There was a photograph of him looking too big and too vital for a leather armchair, his light hair contrasting with a dark background, two buttons of his shirt casually undone, and captioned, *Dain Ransome, seen here relaxing in one of the city's plushest hotels, says he feels more at home roughing it in a tent—on ice. Here, only the drinks come that way ...*

He had a glass of something in his hand, and looked relaxed and pleased with life. So Val had managed to get him to pose for a photograph as well, Kerin thought with envy. Had they gone straight to his hotel after the talk? And how long had Val taken to glean all the information she had packed into the article? There was plenty of it. His childhood on a backblocks farm and his education were described in one or two sentences, then it was on to his passion for geology that had led to a special interest in vulcanology and the publication of his book. He had researched that firsthand in Peru, the Soviet Union, the Philippines and other corners of the world as well as in New Zealand. It was Erebus, the Antarctic's still active volcano, that had first drawn him to the last continent and once there, he admitted, he was 'hooked'.

He had returned to the Antarctic several times between stints lecturing and writing in New Zealand, plus a spell of teaching in a university and a few field trips to other parts of the globe.

'But the Antarctic is my first love,' he says with a grin, Val had written. *Marriage doesn't enter into his plans for the future.* *'There isn't a woman in the world who could rival the Antarctic in beauty and sheer fascination—not to mention a certain amount of capricious bloody-mindedness. Maybe when I'm too old to cope with that, I'll settle down with some cosy, accommodating little woman, who'll warm my slippers and listen to my old man's reminiscences.'*

And what about women in the Antarctic? Mr Ransome acknowledges their presence of recent years but says laconically, *'Basically, the Antarctic is still a man's world.'*

He would! Kerin thought irritably as she put down the paper, not really analysing the reason for her irritation. The force of the man's personality had come through in Val's write-up, and also a little of the fascination that he held—for Val, of course, who had admitted he attracted her even as an image on the TV screen. And the attraction had been mutual, it seemed, if fleeting. For Val's sake, Kerin hoped it was fleeting on *her* side. The man had given fair warning, after all, that no girl should take him seriously. Not if she had permanence in mind ...

She reached for the phone and dialled the number of the paper, asking to be put through to Miss Lamont.

'Congratulations,' she said, when Val's voice came through on the line. 'Your Ransome piece was terrific.'

'Why, thank you, Kerin. You're a good sport! I could hardly believe my luck when he whisked me away like that!'

'The masterful type!' Kerin commented drily.

Val chuckled. 'Definitely! I have a confession to make—
I rather liked it.'

'Traitor! What price the Human Rights Act now?'

'What's that?' Val asked innocently.

'Only the Act that outlaws discrimination against women
—the one you quoted to your boss yesterday, remember?'

'Spoilsport! I'll remember it tomorrow—after Dain goes
away. I'm seeing him tonight—a proper invitation this
time, not a spur-of-the-moment thing. You must admit
he's a dreamy man.'

'Well, don't get too carried away, will you? He's wedded
to his work, by all accounts—by *your* account, at least.'

'Don't worry, I know that. I didn't spend hours with him
on Wednesday without receiving *that* message loud and
clear. He's just back from the ice, and he wants a good
time—that's natural. And I don't mind helping him have
it. At least I'll have a beautiful memory.'

'Where's he going tomorrow?' Kerin asked.

'America. He's doing a lecture tour or something, and
then I gather he's to be attached to one of their universities
for a few months, sort of combination teaching and re-
searching.'

'Nice for him,' Kerin said casually, fighting some foreign
emotion that seemed compounded of disappointment and
relief. 'Well, have a good time.'

'Thanks, I know I will. 'Bye, Kerin.'

She and Roger were going out tonight, too, to a new
film and a late supper afterwards. The dress she planned to
wear was new, silky and clinging with a prettily flared
skirt swirling about her knees. The colour was a rich dark
green that turned her eyes dark and mysterious, and she
played them up as she got ready with a subtle green eye-
shadow and a touch of mascara on the tips of already dark
lashes.

She added a faint dusting of powder to her lightly tanned
skin and a pretty pink gloss to her mouth before donning
a pair of high-heeled black sandals, and surveyed her ap-
pearance in the mirror with satisfaction.

Roger was right on time, and when she opened the door for him his eyes slipped over her with blatant appreciation. He touched his lips to her cheek—he was always considerate, and wouldn't want to spoil her lipstick this early in the evening—complimented her and said, 'Ready?'

'Just about. Come in, Roger.'

Her flatmate wandered out of her bedroom and said casually, 'Oh, hi, Roger.'

'Hello, Cara.' Roger smiled at the girl as Kerin returned to her own room for a fringed silk wrap and a small evening purse, and she could hear their voices as they exchanged pleasantries. Cara liked Roger and in private jokingly pretended jealousy of Kerin for appropriating such a good-looking and successful male. 'If you ever decide to throw him back, throw in my direction, will you?' she had said laughingly, once. 'Not that I suppose you're that crazy.'

It was all in fun, of course, but sometimes Kerin suspected an underlying element of sincerity in Cara's coveting of Roger. Not that she would ever do anything to hurt her friend. Her loyalty to Kerin was unbending, founded on a friendship that went back many years.

The film was not quite up to expectation, but it gave them something to talk about over their supper in a quiet, crowded but attractive little restaurant afterwards. The light was dim, creating an impression of intimacy about their table for two in a corner even though there were at least fifty other people in quite a small space.

They lingered over coffee, and Roger laid his warm hand over hers on the table, stroking her wrist pleasantly with his thumb. She looked up with a slight smile, realising how handsome he was, the feeble flaring of a single low red candle on the table emphasising the classically straight nose, the sensuous shaping of his mouth, the unmistakable light of admiration and desire in his dark eyes.

He lifted her hand—the left one—from the table and began to play with her fingers, running his thumb over them in turn, and stopping at the third one, holding it and smiling into her eyes.

'It looks bare,' he said lightly.

Kerin smiled uncertainly.

He bent his head and dropped a quick kiss on her hand, but didn't let it go. And in that instant as his dark head was lowered, she looked across it and straight into a pair of ice-blue eyes.

Dain Ransome and Val were seated at another table half-way across the room.

'How about putting a ring on it?' Roger was saying, and she stared at him, still feeling the sudden shock of the impact of seeing Dain Ransome look at her without a vestige of recognition.

Roger reached across the small table to take her chin in his thumb and forefinger, tilting her face a little while he still held her left hand in his. '*Well?* Is it so much of a surprise?'

'Yes,' she said, not thinking of him at all. And then, as the sense of what he had said penetrated, she was flooded with sudden shame and remorse. 'Oh, Roger!' she smiled at him with melting warmth to make up for inexcusable inattention at such a crucial moment in their relationship. 'I don't know what to say——'

His fingers left her chin and his face became shuttered.

Remorseful, Kerin put her own hand quickly over the one that still held her left one. 'Let's go,' she said. 'We can't talk here.'

To her relief he was only too ready to accede to the suggestion. He put his arm about her as they left, and she carefully didn't look in the direction of the table where Ransome and Val were sitting. Thank heaven, she thought to herself, Val had been facing the other way.

'Will you come to my place, Kerin?' Roger asked.

'No,' she said. 'Take me home, please. Cara will have gone to bed.'

'Okay.' He sounded a little wry, and she wondered if he thought she didn't trust him. It wasn't that. But she had the feeling that whatever they had to say, she would be some-how at a disadvantage in Roger's own home. He could be very persuasive, and she didn't want to be persuaded into anything she might come to regret.

He refused more coffee when they entered the flat, and pulled her down beside him on the sofa. She started to say, 'Roger——'

But he silenced her with a kiss, parting her lips hungrily and pressing her head against the back of the sofa until she gave in and responded to his passion.

'That's better,' he said huskily, when at last he lifted his head and eased his hold a little, shifting so that she lay back against his shoulder. His lips moving against her temple, he said, 'How about that ring, darling? Shall we buy one on Monday?'

She was silent, and he gave a soft little laugh and said, 'You want a proper proposal? Kerin, will you marry me?'

'It isn't that,' she said. 'I——I just don't know, Roger. You're going a little too fast for me, I think.'

He moved a little, and cupped his hand beneath her chin, turning her to face him. 'Am I?' He seemed a little surprised. 'Have I been over-confident? I thought from the way you responded to me—the way we get on together—that you felt the same way I do.'

'I did—I do—at least, I think I do.'

'*Think!*' His hand dropped, and she looked away, puzzled by her own reactions.

'I didn't expect—this——' Kerin tried to explain. 'At least, not so soon.'

'You're not going to say, "Mr Harris, this is so sudden!" are you?'

She smiled. 'No, of course not.'

'Because it isn't,' he went on. 'And you know it isn't. You must have known—in fact you just admitted as much—that I was planning to marry you.'

'Well—yes. I hoped——'

'Hoped? Oh, darling!'

But she evaded his kiss, pushing away from him. 'Please don't, Roger. I'm just not sure. I need more time.'

He stood up, looking down at her troubled face, his own

chagrined and a little remote. 'Okay. But don't keep me waiting too long, will you? I'm not a boy, Kerin. I'm thirty-seven, and I want—well, I want this thing settled. We've known each other over a year now. We've been working together, seeing each other practically every day. I'd have thought by now you'd be as sure as I am.'

Kerin stood, too. 'I thought I was,' she admitted slowly. 'Maybe I'm just panicking a bit now that—that it comes to the point. Marriage is a big step, Roger.'

'Yes,' he admitted. 'Particularly for a woman, I suppose.' He frowned, trying to be fair. 'I won't be asking you to give up your career, you know,' he said. 'You're too good a journalist for that.' He grinned, trying to lighten the atmosphere. 'I'd hate to lose you from my staff! But I'd hope for children some time. Maybe you could part-time for a while, or do some freelancing from home.'

'Between washing nappies and wiping noses?' she asked, a faint edge to her teasing tone. 'Do you see me as the mother of your children, Roger?'

His mouth tautened a little, and he said, 'Yes. Yes, I do.'

His hands grasped her shoulders and pulled her to him to receive his kiss, possessive and forceful. His arms slipped about her body, and he said huskily, 'Don't panic, darling. We'll both lose some of our freedom, but it will be worth it, I promise you. We'll have a good marriage.' He kissed her again, and, wanting to believe him, Kerin pressed close and offered her lips willingly to his. She let his hands explore her body through the fine material of her dress, and then he lifted his head a little and she opened her eyes to see him looking down at her with a peculiar intentness.

A sudden look of decision came into his eyes, then she closed hers as his mouth sought hers, and felt his hands moving across her back until they found her zip and began to ease it down.

She stiffened and moved her head a little in a small movement of denial. It had always been enough before, but this time Roger ignored her rejection, continuing to kiss her with slow, deliberate expertise while the zip slid down with surprising speed, and his hands eased the dress from her shoulders and caressed their bared outlines.

In that moment she wanted him very much, and she thought, *why not*? Perhaps it would help to resolve her doubts.

He slipped his thumb under the strap of her bra and eased it out of the way as his lips trailed across her shoulder. His sleek dark hair brushed against her cheek, and she turned her head to look at it, recalling with sudden clarity the moment in the restaurant when he had bent over her hand and she had looked up to see Dain Ransome watching them with his coldly indifferent blue eyes.

Desire suddenly washed away, and she saw, as though through *his* watching eyes, herself in Roger's arms, her dress slipping from her shoulders, her half-closed eyes glazed with surrender to passion.

The picture seemed very sordid, and instinctively she strained against Roger's hold, the melting willingness suddenly changing to frantic rejection.

Too suddenly for Roger. His hands tightened, becoming almost cruel, and he muttered against her throat, 'Don't fight me, stop panicking, darling. I won't hurt you.' And then, '*Dammit*, Kerin, I *want* you!'

She cried, 'No!' and wrenched herself away with some violence, straightening her dress with shaking fingers as he stepped back and looked at her furiously.

'For God's *sake*!' he snapped. 'There's no need to yell. Do you want to wake Cara?'

'I'm sorry, Roger,' she said. 'You'd better go.'

He looked ready to argue, but after a moment shrugged and said, 'All right. You're not going to give me an answer tonight?'

'I can't. Please leave it, now.'

He went, not very pleased, and Kerin sighed and got ready for bed. The evening had been traumatic, and it was difficult to sleep. She wished that Roger had waited a little longer, before asking her to marry him. Which was silly, because as he had said, she had expected him to do it, he had given her unmistakable hints of what was in his mind. She didn't know what had come over her. Usually she was a decisive person, not a bit dithery, even about important decisions. She had even been sure in her mind, before it all happened, that when Roger did propose she would accept him. If she had not been planning to do so she would never have encouraged him so far. It wasn't her first proposal, but scalp-hunting had never been her line, and if she thought a man was getting serious she had always tried to break off the relationship before he got in too deeply. With Roger, she had been serious herself.

So why this sudden, unexpected doubt?

Dain Ransome, came the answer, unbidden, into her mind. But that was ridiculous. She had more sense than to let a passing attraction for a man she didn't even know influence her actions.

Still, she wasn't sorry that the thought of his cold eyes had stopped what she had allowed Roger to begin tonight. She was a little ashamed of her motives for allowing him to go so far. And she had a distinct feeling that Roger had made a rather cold-blooded decision to try and make her commit herself to him fully.

Their mutual desire had been real enough, but underlying it had been a mixture of emotions and hopes that seemed somehow a little unedifying. Roger said he loved her, and she was almost sure she loved him, and yet that interlude of passion had had less to do with sharing their love than with his need to make sure of her, and hers to be sure of herself. Although it had been seen by both of them as a possible way of resolving their problems, they had both, in a way, been using each other.

Roger's manner to her didn't change. He was still charming and considerate and he kissed her after their frequent outings with the same sensuous expertise as before. Perhaps she was imagining the slightly proprietorial air which he seemed to have adopted lately, she thought, as she packed a small case preparatory to going with him to spend a weekend with his parents. 'No strings,' he had told her, issuing the invitation. 'My parents are the old-fashioned sort.'

They lived in Queenstown, a beautiful tourist resort that occupied a choice position on a series of gentle slopes between the breathtaking beauty of Lake Wakatipu and the snowy grandeur of a range of mountains appropriately named the Remarkables.

The plane that flew them down wasn't big, but the weather was fine all the way, and when they arrived the town looked drowsily pretty, the exotic trees still holding flame and gold colours of autumn, and mountains mantled in white in the background. Roger's mother and father welcomed her warmly, and although nothing was said, their glances seemed to approve of her in a particularly personal way, and she had no doubt that Roger had indicated to them she might one day become a member of the family. Their house, overlooking the lake with its surrounding bush-covered hills, was a restful place, but on the Sunday she was glad when Roger took her to the ski-fields for the day. She was not an expert skier, but competent enough not to disgrace him—he was pretty good, himself, and they had a thoroughly enjoyable day.

As they drove back to his parents' house she felt more in accord with him than she had for a long time, and when he put out his hand and squeezed her fingers in his, she reciprocated with a natural, affectionate smile.

They returned to Christchurch early the following morning, and as he drove into the city from the airport Roger said quietly, not taking his eyes from the road, 'I'm still waiting for an answer from you, Kerin.'

She almost said yes, there and then, because surely she was going to, eventually, and what was the point of keeping him waiting? But something held her back. 'I know,' she told him. 'Please be patient a little longer, Roger.'

He cast her a wry, curious glance and didn't answer.

For something to do, she began to flip through the paper they had purchased at the airport, not really reading, just glancing at headlines. She went right through to the Situations Vacant columns, and Roger flashed a glance at the page and asked mildly, 'Thinking of leaving me?'

'No, of course not,' she said, laughing a little. She looked down and saw a heading in bold type: *ANTARCTIC*. And below that:

Men and women wanted for next season's Antarctic teams. Surveyors, geologists, scientists required. Also radio-operator, carpenter, cook and dog-handler. Applications also invited for the position of Information Officer, background in journalism or public relations preferred. Apply in the first instance to . . .

'Kerin?' Roger said sharply.

'What?'

'I asked if you want to drop by the flat before we go to the office.'

'Oh—no, thanks.'

She closed the paper and folded it carefully. Her heart was beating fast, and she felt breathless, with a stirring of excitement.

Antarctica—a frozen continent, an icy wasteland at the uttermost perimeter of the earth. A snowbound, blizzard-swept, hostile environment where men and a very few women survived and worked by the sweat of their brows and the skin of their teeth, and their own ingenuity that allowed them to keep, most of the time, a step ahead of the inimical climate.

Antarctica—a place that could make a man give up the comforts of civilisation, the satisfaction and safety of a secure career, the possibility of a settled home with a wife and family while he was young enough to enjoy them.

And suddenly the restlessness that had plagued her, the trapped feeling that had pursued her and almost stifled her this weekend in the Harrises' lovely lakeside home, to be dispelled only by the hours spent on the white mountainside with its covering of crisp snow, its free space and pure cold air, crystallised and shattered all at once.

Suddenly she knew exactly and most specifically what she wanted.

She wanted to go to Antarctica.

CHAPTER THREE

IT wasn't just as easy as that, of course. She was interviewed, after her letter of application was received, by the superintendent of the Antarctic Division, and then interviewed again.

The second time another man was present, introduced as Professor Prince, who was from the university. The first interview had centred on her experience in journalism, but now it seemed they were interested in another aspect of her application. Among the qualifications (academic) she had listed in the appropriate section of her application form, she had put everything she could think of, hoping to impress. It seemed that she had.

'You have a degree in psychology?' the superintendent asked her.

'Yes. After I left university I worked in industrial psychology for six months. Then I went overseas for eighteen months, and as I was moving about a lot, had to give up that type of work, planning to take it up later when I returned to this country. But while I was travelling about I began writing travel articles and other short pieces for magazines and newspapers, and found that I enjoyed that, and was quite successful. When I came back I took a short course in journalism at a technical college, and I've been doing that ever since, first for a suburban newspaper, and now for *Adventure* magazine.'

'Miss Paige,' the Professor leaned forward, 'have you any experience of living in rough conditions with a small group of people?'

'Well—yes,' she said, telling him about the camping trip with four other people through some of the lesser known parts of the world, and the Pacific yacht cruise.

The Professor leaned back thoughtfully. 'Did you find

34

those situations stressful?' He had penetrating blue eyes, in a thin face. His stooped shoulders might have denoted physical frailty, but his mind, she could see, was as strong as anyone's.

She thought about his question, and said, 'No. There were some strains, of course, in a small group of people living closely together. But in both cases we weathered those successfully. I found it much more enjoyable than stressful.'

'But in both cases the companions were known to you— they were personal friends before you went off together on these—adventures.'

'Yes. And if I go to the Antarctic, I'll be among strangers.'

'Correct. The circumstances are different. You realise that most of these strangers will be men? Does that appeal to you?'

A dry note had entered his voice, and she looked at him frankly, trying to appraise the purpose of the question. 'Doing a job in the Antarctic appeals to me,' she said slowly. 'And it would, whoever my fellow-workers happened to be.'

The superintendent looked approving, she thought, and the Professor turned to him and gave a small nod.

The superintendent cleared his throat, and said, 'I'm going to leave you with the Professor for a while. Would you please answer his questions as fully as you can, Miss Paige.'

She did as he asked to the best of her ability, and after half an hour or so the superintendent returned and looked questioningly at the other man. Receiving a nod, he turned to Kerin and said, 'Thank you for being patient with us, Miss Paige. The thing is, we have rather a special proposition to put to you. For some years, Professor Prince here has been interviewing the men—and lately the women, who have wintered over at the Antarctic stations. He would really like some first-hand expert observation, but so far that hasn't been possible. Even more'—the

superintendent looked slightly embarrassed—'he would
prefer that the men—and women, of course—are not—reminded that their psychological reactions are being ex-
amined.'

'You mean, you don't want them to know?' Kerin asked
bluntly, looking directly at the Professor.

- 'My dear young lady——' he said, smiling gently. 'You
must know very well that when people know they're being
observed, their behaviour patterns become subject to
changes which would not occur otherwise. You know from
your training that that is one of the most frustrating ob-
stacles faced by psychological observers trying to collect
accurate empirical data on the behavioural patterns of the
human race. Unfortunately we often have to have recourse
to a certain amount of subterfuge.'

'Some of which is downright immoral,' said Kerin. 'Like
asking one person to administer electric shocks to another.'

'Ah, yes, the famous—or infamous—experiment,' the
Professor murmured. 'But do remember, won't you, the
persons apparently suffering the shocks *were* only faking
their pain.'

'I still think it was horrible,' Kerin said stubbornly.

'Yes, well—it taught us some interesting things about
human nature. And I don't think that what we're going to
ask you to do is immoral. These people will be told that
they are being asked to take part in a psychological programme, and will be interviewed at the end of the year—
this is standard practice already, and no one has objected
so far. They're scientists themselves, and they understand
the need for information, data, records. They'll be asked to
keep a record of their own, which at the end will be compared with the detailed observations of a trained observer.'

'I'm hardly *that*!' Kerin objected.

'Of course you are!' said the Professor. 'A little rusty,
perhaps, but I'll give you a crash course to bring you up to
date and tell you exactly what it is I want, before you go.'

'You applied for the job of Information Officer, of
course,' the other man put in. 'We have other applications,

in fact a great many, and some of them very highly qualified and very able people. It's your psychological qualification that makes you unique, Miss Paige. If you agree to help out Professor Prince, the job of Information Officer is yours. There'll be extra pay, of course, in consideration. It's always useful when one person can do two jobs in the Antarctic, it means we can send more bodies. The accommodation is limited, and versatility and adaptability are always prime considerations.'

He looked at her questioningly and said, 'You may think it over for a couple of days, if you like.'

But the choice was quite clear. She either agreed to do both jobs or she didn't go. There were better people than her queueing for the post of Information Officer. It was only because she could do the Professor's observations for him that she was being offered a place on the team at all.

'I'll take it,' she said.

Telling Roger was the hardest part. At first he was stunned, then furious.

'You might have told me!' he exclaimed, rising from his chair behind his desk as she stood before him.

'It might never have happened,' she said. 'Hundreds of people apply for those jobs. There was no point in upsetting you if I didn't get it.'

'Upsetting me! Well, yes, I suppose you could say I'm upset!' he said sarcastically. 'Good God, girl! I've asked you to marry me, you've kept me dangling for weeks, and now you calmly come in and tell me you're going to the bloody Antarctic for a year! Is this why you've been stalling me off? If you hadn't got the job, would you have settled for second-best—marriage to me?'

'No!' Kerin cried. 'It wasn't like that, Roger. I applied for the job after you asked me to marry you, after that weekend at your parents' place, in fact——'

. He laughed bitterly. 'I thought we were so close that weekend,' he said.

'Oh, we were!' she assured him. 'I felt that, too.'

'Then why?' He flung out a hand in exasperated despair. 'This is my answer, isn't it? *Isn't* it?' he insisted. 'You've finally given me an answer and it's *no*.'

'Yes,' she said quietly, 'I suppose it is.'

'You suppose!' He came round the desk and gripped her by the arms, looking down at her. 'You surely don't expect me to wait for you!'

Bravely she met his eyes. 'No,' she said. 'That wouldn't be fair.'

'Well, at least you recognise that!'

'I'm sorry, Roger,' she said inadequately. 'Truly sorry.'

'Are you? It doesn't help, you know.'

Helplessly, she said, 'I know. But what else can I say? I can't even ask you to understand—I don't really understand it myself. But it's something I feel very deeply, Roger —this is something I must do.'

'You don't love me,' he said flatly.

Hesitantly she said, 'Not enough, obviously. Please don't think too badly of me. I did want it to work out, for us.' She put her hands to his lapels and looked down, her eyes filling with tears. 'I'll miss you, Roger.'

He muttered, '*Kerin!*' and pulled her into his arms, kissing her with a kind of desperate passion.

She kissed him back, and he insisted, 'You *do* care for me.' And she said, 'Yes.'

'I won't let you go,' he said, and kissed her again until she was dizzy and breathless, breaking away from him with an effort.

'But I have to!' she insisted. 'Please don't make it hard for me, Roger.'

'Hard! I'll damn well make it impossible!' he said, hauling her back into his arms.

But this time she fought him, and in the end he let her go, frustrated rage in his face, in his voice, as he said, 'I don't understand you, Kerin.'

'Please,' she said tiredly. 'Just leave it, Roger. I'll work out my notice and then when I come back I'll find another job. I'm sorry it had to end this way.'

She was almost at the door when he said, in a strained voice, 'It doesn't have to end.'

She turned and said a little desperately, 'Roger, I won't change my mind. I'm going.'

He looked grim and a trifle flushed. 'All right, I accept that, you're a very determined girl. Maybe it's something you have to work out of your system—you've always been drawn to adventure—if you weren't you wouldn't want to work for this magazine. I think you're still panicking, Kerin, running away from—from marriage, I suppose. You're scared of settling down, of losing your freedom, aren't you?'

'Maybe I am, a bit,' she admitted. 'But that's only part——'

'Okay,' he said quickly. 'Look, I felt the same way, but I'm older, ready to make a go of it. Perhaps I've been too impatient with you. You just admitted that you care for me. I still want to buy you that ring, Kerin. I want you to wear it—and, when you come back, either hand it back, or add a wedding ring to it.'

'Oh, Roger, thank you!' she said, deeply touched. 'But it wouldn't be fair to you!'

He strode over to take her hands. 'It's what I want,' he said. 'You've been full of doubts. I have a feeling when you come back you'll have sorted out just what you do feel for me, one way or the other. We won't make any announcements, but I'd like you to be wearing my ring, and I promise I won't hold you to it if you—decide against me.' He bent and gently kissed her lips. 'Please—do this for me.'

The ring Roger bought her was a large diamond flanked by smaller emerald chips. When Kerin protested at the size of the stones, Roger grinned and said, 'I want all those guys at the Pole to know that you're booked—at least, until you get home,' he added with a touch of anxiety. That hint of unsureness was unlike his usual suavity and self-confidence, and she smiled back at him and touched his hand briefly and didn't argue any more. She knew he could afford the slightly ostentatious ring, and if that was what he was determined to give her, she would accept it to please him. She was working hard at pleasing him these days, well aware that it was because she felt guilty—guilty about her uncertainty, her leaving him, and allowing him to talk her into wearing the symbol of an intended marriage that might never take place.

It wasn't until she was trying on her Antarctic gear, during a hilarious session in the flat with Cara, that she realised the size of the ring defeated Roger's avowed purpose. It was decidedly uncomfortable and very nearly impossible to wear under the regulation two pairs of gloves or gloves and mittens. She would be wearing them most of the time, she gathered, and the ring would have to be left behind whenever she ventured outside the base buildings.

Anyway, she decided, as she grinned back at Cara, convulsed by the sight of her muffled up in layers of clothing starting with cream wool long johns and long-sleeved top, a down jacket and matching trousers over them, topped finally by a windproof parka and baggy windproof trousers, and her canvas-and-rubber mukluks worn over two pairs of heavy woollen socks, a balaclava over her head and snow-goggles over eyes, dressed like this she was hardly likely to awake lust in any man. They would scarcely even be aware that she was a woman!

'Actually,' she said, 'they told us that in summer you don't need to wear everything all at once, unless there's a wind.'

'Summer?' Cara repeated sceptically.

'All the way from November to March, and the temperature sometimes rises above freezing point.'

'*Sometimes!*' Cara raised her eyes heavenwards, then watched thoughtfully as Kerin stripped off her cumbersome gear. 'Why are you doing it?' she asked seriously. 'Roger's just given you that super ring, and now you're off to literally the ends of the earth.'

'It's difficult to explain,' Kerin confessed.

'But Roger understands?'

Kerin glanced up briefly from folding her parka and said, 'No. No, he doesn't understand, Cara. But he asked me to wear his ring, all the same.'

'You're a very lucky girl, Kerin.' Cara's voice shook a little, and Kerin looked up to find the other girl's face faintly flushed and a little indignant. She was angry for Roger's sake, and Kerin couldn't blame her. On impulse, she bent and kissed her friend's cheek.

'I know that,' she said gently. 'I know I don't deserve him, Cara.'

Packing her gear was the last task in the long process of preparation. There had been health checks, which she had been relieved to pass with flying colours, injections, and purchases to make. Some gear was provided by the department, but a lot had to be bought specially. She had been kept busy, too, by Professor Prince's special sessions with her, and then there had been the week-long orientation and training course where she had the chance to meet the other members of the party. Some of them were 'summer people' who would leave before the continent became shut off in the Antarctic winter while the hard core 'wintered over.'

There was some surprise that the Information Officer was to be one of the winter team; it wasn't usual. But the official story was the department had commissioned her to write a book. They were going to be the first team at a new station, and the department wanted a full official record in readable form which would be made available to the public.

There was one other woman in the party, a biologist. Rose Carson was in her thirties, a little overweight and cheerfully aware that in her padded clothing she looked even more clownish than the rest of them, for she stood only five feet two in her boots. Kerin found her good fun, and the men, too, seemed a friendly crowd. Some of them made no secret of the fact that they were going to enjoy having the women along, although she noticed that some of the 'old hands' seemed a trifle put out.

There were lectures on Antarctic geology and ecology, and first aid, safety and survival, and practical training in erecting Antarctic tents and negotiating snowfields, on the slopes of Mount Ruapehu, one of the North Island's popular ski centres. Instead of staying at the 'Chateau'—the large tourist hotel that graced the slopes of the mountain—they were billeted at the nearby Waiouru army camp. On a high, barren plateau swept by winds from the mountains, it was a cold, bleak place, approximating the conditions they could expect in the Antarctic.

Their leader was a big, bluff ex-army man called Bill Boyes, with a friendly manner that combined humour and benign authority. He would be in charge of twenty New Zealanders and fifteen Americans and carry the official title of Commander, Hillary Station. The Americans they would meet at the station itself. International co-operation was a big thing in Antarctica, and the two nations had successfully run a joint station at Hallett for many years. The new station was a rather bigger venture, smaller than Scott Base, New Zealand's main Antarctic station, but bigger than any of the others. In many ways it was innovative.

When the day of embarkation finally arrived Kerin woke early with an immediate fluttering of excitement in her stomach. The adventure was about to begin.

Cara came into her room, carrying a bulky parcel. 'Here,' she said. 'I bought you something.'

'Oh, Cara! Thank you.'

She sat on the bed and opened it, shaking out a fleecy-lined stretch nylon ski-suit—figure-hugging red pants and a jacket to match.

'I know you have to wear those ghastly padded things when it gets really cold,' Cara told her. 'But I saw this and it looked so smart—and it *is* quite warm, see?' She touched the soft lining. 'I thought you might like to wear it in the plane. It's very smart—much nicer than those awful baggy things.'

'Those awful baggy things', Kerin knew, had been de-signed that way to keep in body heat, but she was touched by the gift and she donned the suit over her long undies and a natural wool jersey before Roger called to take her to the airport.

Cara came along too, and she kissed them both goodbye, a peck on the cheek and a hug for Cara, and a quick kiss on the mouth for Roger—but he caught her close and kissed her thoroughly until she broke away, pink-cheeked and avoiding his eyes. Cara was carefully looking another way, but there were one or two interested glances from a couple of men she had met at Waiouru. Their clothing made it obvious who they were, and she couldn't help wondering if Roger was staking his claim deliberately.

The formalities were tedious and time-consuming, and there was some goodnatured grumbling among some members of the party, but at last the cumbersome Hercules lifted off and they were on their way.

'I say, that's very glamorous!' Rose Carson told her as she undid her seat belt beside Kerin, and ran a slightly doubtful eye over the red suit.

'But impractical,' Kerin smiled. 'It was a gift, and I didn't want to hurt the person who gave it to me by not wearing it. Are you looking forward to Hillary?'

Rose grimaced. 'I was, but it seems I'm not headed for there now. I've been transferred to Scott Base.'

'Really? Why?'

The other woman shrugged. 'Ours not to reason why,' she said with humorous resignation. 'That's what the powers that be decided. I don't mind too much. It's still the Antarctic, after all.'

Kerin agreed, and looked about the plane, picking out familiar faces.

'Only a few of our lot—*your* lot, I should say, on this flight,' Rose commented.

'Yes, I don't recognise many of these people,' said Kerin. 'I know Bill and some of the others were to go with the first flight after the winter. Bill said they'd be leaving about the beginning of October.'

In front of them, a man she vaguely recognised twisted round to speak to them. 'Excuse me——' he said. 'Hallo, Rose—Kerin.'

They returned the greeting, and he said, 'Heard you mention Bill. Didn't you know what's happened?'

'What?' Rose asked.

The man grinned. 'It's funny, really. Bill's been through the Vietnam war, climbed mountains when he had nothing better to do, tracked across the Antarctic and once went down a crevasse and got hauled out without a scratch. Then a couple of weeks back he walked down his own back steps in the dark, tripped over his feet and broke a leg.'

'I don't suppose he's laughing,' Rose said a little drily.

'Guess not,' their informant admitted. 'By the way, my name's Les Howard, in case you've forgotten.'

The man clicked into place in Kerin's brain, and she recalled that he was one of those who had spent a season in the Antarctic already. He was to winter over this time.

'You're a surveyor, aren't you?' she asked.

'That's right.' He smiled. It was a nice smile, in a nice, craggy, comfortable-looking face. 'Do you know we kiwis have mapped more than ninety thousand square miles of the Antarctic? I aim to finish the job.'

'Alone?' Kerin laughed.

'If necessary. Seriously, though, there's a long way to go, but there's something about being a part of something that big. You know, I'll probably be long dead and gone by the time they finish the job, but it gives me satisfaction just to know that I did my small bit.'

Rose said, 'If Bill's out of action, who's going to take over as leader at Hillary?'

'One of the best,' said Les with satisfaction. 'Some reckon he's a bit of a martinet, but I think that's only because he won't stand for slacking or carelessness, and I'm all for a bit of discipline myself, when people get careless in the Antarctic. Carelessness costs lives, down on the ice, and it's just as well to have a leader who doesn't let anyone forget it. We'll be all right with him.'

'What's his name?' Kerin asked, quite unaware of the bombshell that was about to explode about her ears.

And Les said casually, 'Ever heard of Dain Ransome?'

CHAPTER FOUR

HOURS later, looking down at the first distant, broken patches of white that littered the South Polar Sea far below, Kerin wondered why she hadn't been more surprised.

Dain Ransome was supposed to have been in America, she thought. There had been no suggestion that he was to spend another summer on the ice so soon. And yet after the first shock when she heard his name, she had experienced only a feeling of inevitability.

With luck, he might even have forgotten her. And even if he hadn't, surely a man of his reputation and experience was too big to let a single tactless remark affect his attitude to one of the people under his command. He had snubbed her thoroughly once, and wouldn't he think that was punishment enough? Even if he did recognise her, she would count on his being willing to wipe clean the slate and start afresh. According to Les, he was to be both summer and winter leader, not handing over as some did after six months. A grudge couldn't last a year.

They landed at Williams Field near Scott Base, Erebus smoking gently in the distance, were welcomed and then bundled into sno-tracks for a bumpy ride to the long line of flat-roofed huts linked by half-round corrugated iron passageways. Just in front of the base the blunt-nosed machine lurched across a pressure-ridge in the ice with a sickening lunge, and finally came to rest close to the ramp at the base entrance.

The sun was shining and it was like a balmy winter's day. In the base itself they doffed the parkas they had put on before landing and were shepherded over the slippery duck-boards of a covered way to the insulated warmth of the mess, where they enjoyed a delicious and hearty meal.

Then Kerin and Les and five others said goodbye to

Rose and their other travelling companions and climbed on board another Hercules, this time equipped with skis for the journey to the other side of the Ross Ice Shelf. The shelf, a thick layer of ice covering the sea, was in area about the same size as France, five hundred and twenty thousand square kilometres, only a small corner of a vast continent. But in adverse weather they would be cut off completely from their nearest 'neighbours' and thrown entirely on their own resources.

For a time they could see the broken coast with its ice-bergs, floating white islands drifting lazily out to sea against inky water. Les leaned across from where he sat beside Kerin and pointed to black, slug-shaped objects lying on the white snow near the water and said, 'Seals.'

She watched the white landscape below in fascination, seeing vast tracts of virgin snow, and sometimes unexpected patterns, no sign of movement, of life.

Then they were landing, and she put on her parka again, pulling up the fur-lined hood, donned her gloves and mittens and followed Les from the plane, keeping herself behind his considerable bulk.

At a little distance she could see the buildings, similar to the ones at Scott, and with a plethora of odd masts and wires extending into the air from the roofs of some of the huts. A couple of sno-tracks and some sleds stood nearby, and there was even a dog team, adding what she thought of as a touch of authenticity to the Antarctic scene. Several men were about, and stores were already being unloaded from the plane and piled on some of the sleds.

Then a tall figure with a clipboard in a mittened hand approached them, and somehow the group from the plane arranged itself into a single line, Kerin standing between Les and another man, her heart beating hard and almost painfully in her chest.

He pushed back the hood of his parka and fair hair, a little longer than when she had last seen it, glinted in the sun. He was still clean-shaven, although some of the men about were sporting stubbly growth on their chins.

He gave them all a tight smile, his eyes skimming briefly over them, and said, 'I'm Dain Ransome. Perhaps you'll give me your names as I get to you.'

He held out his hand to the first man in line, who said, 'Jude Lawson, Commander. Geo-chronologist.'

'Not your first stint, is it? Glad to have you with us, Lawson.'

He had a word for Ian Mackintosh, radio engineer, and Sebastian Wright, a young biologist who admitted with a grin to being an Antarctic greenhorn, and an encouraging smile for Dermot Davies, a geologist who said something about being honoured to work with Ransome.

Then he came to Les Howard, and clapped him on the shoulder as they shook hands. 'Les! Good to see you. How's Theresa? And the boys?'

'Great, thanks. You should have come over to see us when you were back in New Zealand.'

'It was a rush this time, Les. After this stint, maybe.'

'I'll hold you to that.'

Then he turned to Kerin, who had been standing with her face shadowed by the fur hood, her gloved hand fiddling with its edges. The blue eyes registered blank shock as she lifted her head and dropped her hand, and the hood fell back from her dark hair. His hand dropped and she didn't dare offer hers. Then his mouth moved, but it was more a snarl than a smile. He said, 'Are you following me?' very softly, then he stepped past her and held out his hand to the last man in the line.

'Guy Halsey—field assistant,' the young man said.

'That means dogsbody about here,' Ransome said pleasantly. 'I hope you're not afraid of work, Halsey.'

'No, sir.'

Cold eyes swept over Kerin who stood quivering with rage, and passed on to Les. He handed the clipboard to the other man and said, 'You know the ropes, Les. Would you tick off those names for me, and check the baggage off? And if you'—his eyes swept over the group— 'would all collect your baggage as it's unloaded, and let

Les know when you've got the lot, you can hitch a ride on the next vehicle heading back to base. Then, if you wait with your bags in the mess hall, someone will show you all your rooms.'

Les went off and the blue eyes turned back again to Kerin. 'Miss—Paige?'

'Yes.'

'When you have your bags and get to the base, I'd like to see you in my office. Anyone at the station will tell you where to find it.'

He turned away before she had a chance to reply and strode off to one of the sno-tracks, which had a sled hitched on behind that was almost full already. A few minutes later the machine took off for the station buildings, its caterpillar tyres making wide tracks in the snow.

Guy Halsey, a tall young man with unruly dark hair and a thin, bony face, said, 'I'm going to see if I can hitch a ride with the dog team. Think it's possible?'

'The boss-man said the next vehicle that leaves,' Kerin shrugged. 'A dog-sled's vehicle, isn't it?'

They both rode it in the end, after introducing themselves to Nat Mitchell, who handled the team with expert hands and strange commands as the dogs pulled with lolling tongues and misted breath over the snow.

It wasn't a fast ride, but the novelty of it more than made up for that. Kerin would have loved it, if it hadn't been for the lump of trepidation that seemed to have lodged somewhere in her throat.

As they removed their baggage outside the station buildings, she asked the dog-handler where to find Dain Ransome's office. Might as well get it over with, she was thinking as she dumped her things in the large room where some of the others were already waiting and went out into one of the covered ways, careful to close the two huge metal doors behind her, and repeat the process in reverse when she entered the building housing Dain Ransome's office. Each building had its own ante-chamber which acted like a submarine airlock to keep the living quarters insulated from the cold. The handles were difficult to use with gloves and were wrapped about with bandages and tape. It puzzled her until she recalled being warned not to touch any metal with bare hands in sub-zero temperatures, as it would stick to the skin. Unwary fingers on a frozen metal door-handle might end with all the skin ripped off.

She hung her parka on a hook in the ante-room and found the door she had been told to look for. It was warm here, and she unzipped her jacket before knocking on the painted wood.

'Come in,' Dain Ransome called, and she took a deep breath and opened the door. This one had an ordinary round handle, and although it felt cold to her ungloved hand, there was no danger where the heating system was operating.

It was a small office, with metal shelves on three walls filled with books and files, two filing cabinets under a small double-glazed window, and a large desk in one corner, against which Dain Ransome was leaning. He wore a dark, close-fitting jersey that emphasised his blond good looks, and his windproof cotton trousers had been replaced by a pair of well-worn jeans that clung to well-muscled thighs and long legs.

'Miss Paige,' he said, glancing at her and then down at a paper he held in his hand. 'Kevin Paige?'

'Kerin,' she corrected him automatically. It was a common mistake that she was accustomed to people making, the penalty of having an unusual name.

He suddenly straightened up and thrust towards her the paper he held, so that she had to take it from his hand. 'That's not what this says,' he said tersely.

She looked down at the page and saw it was headed, PAIGE, KEVIN DALE: JOURNALIST—INFORMATION OFFICER. Beneath it was listed her date of birth and her qualifications, followed by a brief summary of the information she had supplied about herself for the job application.

She looked up and said levelly, 'A typing error. It happens all the time.'

'Not to me, it doesn't,' he said grimly. 'The thing is, *Miss* Paige, I never guessed you were a female.' He twitched the paper out of her fingers again and looked down at it with apparent disgust. 'Kevin Dale Paige,' he read out, and then flicked the paper with fingers as he listed, 'Journalist on *Adventure* magazine; experience—crewing round Pacific, travel across Libya, Tunisia, Algeria, Morocco, worked around Europe, odd jobs, including farmwork, and in England, ticket-collecting, driving hire-cars and working in a holiday camp. Returned home overland by jeep, through Iran, Afghanistan—and the rest. Interests—scuba diving, yachting, skiing, books and people.'

He threw the paper down on the desk, and she said, 'You know, the days are gone when we women sat at home with our knitting while you men did all the interesting things, Mr Ransome.'

'Obviously. But the day has not yet come, Miss Paige, when I have to accept a woman on my team.'

'*What?*' Whatever she had expected, it had not been this, although the signs, she realised had been there for anyone to read.

'I *said*, I'm not having a woman on my team,' he told her in a rock-hard voice. Then his tone changed a little. 'I'm sorry about the mistake, but when that plane turns round you're going to be on it, Miss Paige. Maybe they can find something for you at Scott, otherwise there's still time to fly you home——'

'Mistake!' she interrupted him furiously. 'The only mistake is yours, Mr Ransome. I'm not flying home—and I'm not going back to Scott Base, either.'

'I happen to be the station commander, in case it's escaped your notice,' he said coldly. 'And I say you're going!'

'It's obviously escaped *your* notice,' she said witheringly, 'that we happen to be living in the twentieth century, even here in your so-called man's world. You've buried yourself up to the neck in your precious snow and ice too long,

Commander! There happens to be a Human Rights Act in New Zealand, and it applies to the Ross Dependency like other New Zealand laws. It outlaws discrimination against women in employment among other things, Mr Ransome. You can't refuse to have me on the grounds of my sex.'

'Can't?' His head shifted a little, his strong chin lifting, his eyes narrowed.

'*Can't*, Mr Ransome.'

He looked down at her and suddenly laughed jeeringly, his eyes passing over her slim figure in the clinging red pants and the creamy jersey under the unzipped jacket. 'If necessary I'll toss you over my shoulder and put you on that plane bodily,' he told her.

Physically, of course, he was quite capable of it. 'You do,' she said, 'and I'll add assault to the other charges I'll be bringing against you.'

'Bring what charges you like,' he shrugged. 'I'll answer them when I get back to New Zealand—after the winter. At least I'll be rid of you while we get on with what we have to do.'

But she wasn't beaten yet, by a long chalk. 'Well,' she said, trying to sound confident, 'at least that gives me plenty of time.'

'To prepare your case?'

'To make sure *you* never work in the Antarctic again,' she said deliberately.

It was only a second before he said with soft derision, '*You*'d be lucky!'

But she had seen the quick wariness in his eyes before he adopted a look of calculated disbelief, and pressed her advantage. It was hitting below the belt, but she was desperately disappointed and this was the only way she knew to make him back down. 'Not lucky,' she said with determined calm. 'Clever. I'm a journalist, remember. I know how to use the media. While you're stuck down here without a chance of defending yourself, I'll have every journalist in the country howling for your blood. They don't like injustice, and they love a chance to crusade. And I'll give it to them. I'll write my personal story of how the male chauvinist Commander Ransome wouldn't have me on his team on the grounds that I was a woman, I'll go on TV, I'll go to the Human Rights Commission, and I'll release a press statement when I do it. I'll make such an issue of it they'll probably recall you before winter. The department will have been so embarrassed by all the adverse publicity they won't ever dare hire you again. Government departments have to set an example, you see. After this, they won't touch you with a bargepole. Human rights are a sensitive issue right now.'

He listened with a stony face, but she knew she was getting through. He might not be sure whether she could do what she threatened, but she didn't think he would take the risk. She knew what the Antarctic meant to him, and that was her trump card.

When he spoke he wasn't exactly arguing, but his question was hostile. 'And what strings did the clever little lady pull to get this job?'

Angry colour stinging her cheeks, she snapped, 'None!'

He raised a sceptical eyebrow and she said, trying her darnedest to control her anger, 'I applied for the job and I got it.'

'Don't give me that!' he said impatiently. 'Information Officer is a cushy job, and there are always plenty of takers. I know the kind of people that usually get it, and you're not in that class. You have a couple of years of experience and a modicum of competence, you work for a mediocre little magazine as a second-rate hack-writer. You've not only got a plum job at the newest department showplace, you're supposed to winter over as well—though I wouldn't count on that, if I were you!'

Good heavens! she thought. *Haven't they told him?* She was sure Bill had been told about her special role on the team as a sort of undercover psychologist. But it seemed his replacement hadn't been informed of that.

'Have you—have you read all that they sent you about me?' she demanded.

He looked at her suspiciously. 'Yes. Is there something else I should know?'

'It isn't up to me to tell you,' she said primly. Well, she was sure it wasn't, but that '*second-rate hack-writer*' had stung, and she supposed they would tell him sooner or later. Let him find out for himself.

'Tell me what?'

'I just said, it's not up to me——'

He looked as though he wished there was a rack or a thumbscrew handy, but Kerin looked back at him fearlessly, and he said after a moment, 'There'd better be a good reason for that.'

He sounded just about as threatening as he looked, and she said, wishing she felt less intimidated than she did, 'There is.'

His lip curled sarcastically and he said, 'Don't tell me you're from the S.I.S.'

She almost laughed at that, because it was fantastic enough to be funny, but his expression didn't encourage laughter. She asked, really quite curious, 'What would you do—if I *was* from Security Intelligence?'

His eyes narrowed, and he said softly, 'I'd have you out of here so fast you wouldn't have time to know you'd gone. I won't have my people spied on, and there wouldn't be any question then about it's being because you're a woman.'

'I'm not,' she said—and quickly added, 'a spy, I mean.' Too quickly for him to laugh, and she wondered if he had imagined the brief gleam of humour in his eyes.

She wondered what he would think when he found out what she *was* here for. Perhaps he wouldn't think it was very different from spying. Her heart sank. Maybe the longer he remained in the dark, the better.

'No,' he said, 'they wouldn't do that. The Antarctic is the one place on earth where nations work together in an atmosphere of mutual trust and co-operation. It's unique, and our government wouldn't be stupid enough to jeopardise that.'

He stopped and looked at her with speculation. 'Maybe

you have an influential daddy,' he suggested. 'Your father isn't the Minister or something, is he?'

'My father's dead!' she flashed.

'Sorry.' He didn't sound as though he was. 'Well, in these days of women's liberation, as you've just been reminding me, maybe it's Mummy who has the influence,' he said mockingly. 'Or perhaps——' his eyes appraised her with insulting deliberation, '—perhaps someone in the department just couldn't resist a pretty face.'

Her fingers curled into a fist, but hitting him would do no good. She said, 'I don't have to stay and listen to you insulting me, Mr Ransome. I'll go and get someone to show me my room.'

She turned to the door, but she hadn't even reached for the handle when a hard hand gripped her with bruising force and turned her, slamming her back against the door in the same swift, brutal movement.

'You'll go when I say so!' he said between gritted teeth.

She looked up into a face that had paled with contained rage, and realised how close he was. So close that his thighs touched hers, she could see the tensed muscle of his jaw, the length of his lashes as his eyes blazed a warning at her.

A warning—and something else. A sudden, unexpected awareness that matched her own, taking him by surprise just as it had her.

She didn't dare move, standing pinned against the door with his other hand on the panels beside her face, trapping her. Whatever happened now was up to him. They were a man and a woman, and both of them were thoroughly and completely conscious of it. The knowledge hummed between them like an electrical current, both of them aware of the danger that it represented.

Dain Ransome said, 'You won't get any quarter from me. No concessions to your womanhood. Are you sure you want to stay?'

Her answer was husky, but steady, her eyes still meeting his. 'Yes. And I won't ask for any concessions.'

His hand left the door and he slowly moved back, releasing her arm.

'You'd better get back to the mess,' he said.

Before you do something we'll both regret, she finished for him, mentally. Well, at least the shock had been mutual. She opened the door as he took the few steps across the room back to his desk.

Then she turned and said, 'Just one question, Mr Ransome.'

He looked up, and the anger was still in his eyes. 'Yes?'

'Did you ask for Rose Carson to be left at Scott Base—taken off your team?'

Cynically he said, 'You must know the answer to that one, Miss Pankhurst-from-the-media. No comment.'

Kerin was almost out the door before he said, 'I hope you have some decent Antarctic clothing. That outfit could get you in trouble—in more than one sense.'

Making her way back to the mess, she supposed she should have explained the ski-suit, but at the time she was too fed up to do so. Let him think what he liked. She was under no obligation to explain herself to him.

The others had all come in from the plane and were standing about surrounded by their baggage and drinking cups of hot tea or cocoa. Les got her a cup of cocoa from a table in one corner laden with a variety of do-it-yourself ingredients for hot and cold drinks and some cans of beer and soft drinks.

'It's important to drink plenty here,' he told her. 'Humidity is very low, and you need to guard against dehydration.'

Guy Halsey joined them, a glass of beer in his hand. 'Are you friends with the boss?' he asked Kerin.

'Hardly,' she said, and caught a sharp look from Les.

Guy said, 'Just wondered—I suppose he wanted to see you because you're the only woman in the party. Special accommodation, eh?'

'I doubt it,' she said. 'The commander doesn't believe in

special treatment. Neither do I. He wanted to see me because I was a bit of a surprise. According to the dossier they sent him, my name was Kevin.'

Enlightenment suddenly dawned on Les's rugged face, and Guy threw back his head and laughed.

Kerin sipped her cocoa and looked at Les. He had worked with Dain Ransome before, she remembered. 'Why doesn't he like women, Les?' she asked.

The man looked uncomfortable. 'Oh, I wouldn't say that,' he mumbled, and Kerin remembered the friendly enquiries after Theresa and the boys—Les's wife and family, presumably. And Val, being whisked off with Ransome to his hotel. No, one couldn't say he didn't like women, she supposed. He just had archaic views about their proper place in the scheme of things.

Somebody else called Les's attention, and Guy said to her, 'By the way, what was that Ransome said to you at the plane? It sounded like something about following him.'

Kerin managed a smile. 'Nothing,' she said. 'Just a joke.'

Only it wasn't a joke, and no one was laughing. There had been a sting in that bit of wit, the deliberate repetition of the words she had spoken to him when they first met.

Of course he couldn't really imagine she had come here because of him—could he? He must have known she could have no idea that she was likely to find him back in the Antarctic already.

And yet he *had* thought that was why she had come here, for that moment at least, when he had first seen her. And those few minutes of sexual tension in his office could have reinforced that impression.

One thing was certain—she must never again let him have the least inkling that he could affect her that way. The strength and suddenness of her physical reaction to his closeness had taken her by surprise, but forewarned was forearmed. Now she knew what could happen, it was just a matter of avoidance and control. Avoid the man, and control her emotions.

Since he didn't like her any more than she did him, the

first, within the limits of the circumstances, should be relatively easy. As for her emotions, she had had some experience of sexual attraction before, but she had never let her feelings overcome her good sense. Dain Ransome was an unexpected problem, but not an insurmountable one.

CHAPTER FIVE

KERIN awoke to the sudden shrilling of an alarm clock. At home she had never needed one, but here it was a necessity. It had been strange going to bed in broad daylight, and even pulling the dark-lined curtain across the tiny window had not entirely blotted out the intrusive midnight sun.

A reedy shout sounded from the outside, and one of the huskies was barking in the distance. The only other sound was the faint hum of the generator that supplied power for the station. Kerin had been lodged in what she was told was the guest suite, two rooms with two bunks each, one of which she had chosen for her own, and a bathroom which at the moment she had all to herself. Luxury accommodation for this part of the world, but she didn't suppose it was because Dain Ransome had relented on his promise of no concessions. He probably regarded this as segregating his men from her contaminating influence, rather than catering to her need for privacy.

She winced with shock as her bare feet found the floor. The heat that warmed the rooms came from a convector system on the ceiling, and the chill from the frozen ground below still affected the floor. She was glad she had taken the advice given her by the grinning, bearded young man who had volunteered to show her to her room, to sleep in the top bunk.

There was hot water in the little bathroom, but she was careful to be sparing with it, knowing that water was a precious commodity.

She dressed in her long underwear, a pair of green wool trousers and one of her raw wool jerseys, and fleecy sheep-skin boots, then pulled on her parka before making her way through the maze of buildings separated by their covered corrugated iron passageways. Each 'cold-porch' held a different clutter of equipment, depending on the building, but every one held one essential item—a fire extinguisher. Fire was the greatest potential disaster in the Antarctic, the reason for the careful separation of the buildings, and for their being sited at right angles to the prevailing wind.

She reached the mess and stepped into its welcoming warmth. A delicious aroma wafted across the room as she sat down at a table with Guy and the young biologist, Sebastian Wright.

A burly figure with a friendly grin across a broad, tanned face got up from another table and joined them, greeting them with an unmistakable American accent. 'Eddie Priest,' he introduced himself. 'I fly one of them choppers out there,' he explained, jerking a thumb towards the outside. Kerin remembered seeing two red helicopters parked outside the base buildings. 'You guys all from Kiwiland?'

They said yes, but he was obviously more interested in Kerin's answer than in the two men's. 'Which part you from?' he asked, leaning across the table a little.

'Christchurch.'

'Yeah? Good ole Cheechee. Great place, Christchurch, great beer, great broa——' He stopped himself abruptly and looked so embarrassed that Kerin took pity on him.

'Which part of the states are you from?' she asked.

New York State, he told her, obviously relieved, and proceeded with little encouragement to expound on the beauties of it, until the arrival of breakfast. There was fruit juice, porridge, omelette and bacon and toast with marmalade or jam, followed by tea or coffee. Kerin had everything except the porridge, concentrating on the food, although she was aware that she was attracting curious glances from around the room. Aware, too, that Dain Ransome was sitting at a table not far away with Les and two other men.

At the end of the meal he stood up, rapped on a glass for attention and welcomed the new arrivals from yesterday. Apparently they were the last batch, and the station's complement was now complete. He told them to spend the day familiarising themselves with their surroundings, setting up their equipment and getting to know their fellow-Antarcticans.

'I'm sure I don't need to remind you,' he said, his eyes sweeping the room and coming to rest momentarily on Kerin, 'not to interfere with the work other people are doing. The carpenters, in particular, are busy men. The base isn't yet completed. If any of you others have time to spare, they can probably give you a job banging in nails. No union demarcation exists here!'

That got a small laugh, and he added, 'And a special warning for the newchums among you. Don't go wandering away from the base without letting someone know exactly where you're going, and listen to the advice of the old hands. And *never* leave the base alone under any circumstances. On the ice a partner is essential.

'One more thing—if anyone has a problem or a gripe, bring it to me. It's my job to sort them out. Okay—thank you.'

Kerin didn't have any equipment except a couple of cameras and some related gadgets. What she needed to do was collect information about the base, since it was her job to inform visitors who arrived during the season as to what was happening in the base, as well as collating and writing up information for the outside world on the Antarctic programme.

Deciding it would help if she had a guide, she said to Eddie, 'Do you have a helicopter to fly this morning?'

'Nope. Want me to show you round?'

She smiled. 'You're quick on the uptake, Eddie. Sure you've got time?'

'No problem. Better put on your mukluks, though. And gloves.'

They started with the inside, though, with the kitchen right next to the mess. It was decidedly warm, dominated by the huge diesel burning stove. The cook turned out to be an army-trained man, and Kerin learned that the omelette she had just eaten had been made with dried egg.

On the cold-porch, she looked askance at the huge refrigerator in one corner, and Eddie grinned and said, 'That stops the food from freezing.' She looked sceptical, and he said, 'Cross my heart, lady. I'm not putting you on, honest.'

They visited the communications room, where Ian Mackintosh, the radio engineer, was in his element among a mass of complicated knobs, switches and lights, and the wonderfully equipped darkrooms, and then on to the laboratories.

Eddie edged in front of her and eased his shoulder against the door as he went to open it for her, but he didn't have a hope of hiding the almost life-sized poster of a nude blonde girl that adorned the door.

He shrugged sheepishly, and she said, 'It's all right, Eddie. I'm getting used to them.' There had been pin-ups in the mess, a few in the corridors, even one calendar girl in about the only wall space left by the mass of equipment in the radio room, though none of them had been quite as blatant as this.

'The thing is,' Eddie said earnestly, 'men on their own, you know—well, they like to remember that there *are* girls in the world. It's kind of a compensation, you know? Well, I guess no one knew you were coming, Kerin.'

'That's all right. I wouldn't want the men to feel—self-conscious—because of me.'

'That's all right, then. You're okay, Kerin. As a matter of fact,' he dropped his voice as he opened the door and let her pass him, 'I get suspicious when I see a place here with no girls on the wall—it means the scientist is a—well, you know!'

Kerin bit her lip on a grin and went in to admire the laboratory. Two bearded young men conferring over a rock sample shook her hand and welcomed her to the base, and seemed only too pleased to explain the functions of the equipment they used.

They had a quick look at the small sick bay and medical room, passed by the men's ablution block and their sleeping cubicles, where open doors showed a few family snapshots on the walls and a lot more nude pin-ups, from some of which Kerin hastily averted her eyes, and then went through the generator room and the machinery repair shop before venturing outside.

The sun was shining, but a brisk breeze made Kerin glad she had donned her windproof baggy trousers over the green wool slacks. The cold was intense, although some of the carpenters who were putting the finishing touches to the prefabricated buildings were working in plaid shirts with their sleeves rolled up.

There wasn't much to see about the base except the two helicopters, some wide-tracked machines and the cache of fuel for them, and the big incinerators that had been built to cope with the rubbish, and storage sheds. The snow round about was dirty and turning to unpleasant slush, and in places gritty volcanic moraine showed through a thinning cover. But beyond the base, a pristine sheet of soft white spread across the ice towards the sea, and in the other direction, past the pressure ridges that formed where the ice pushed against the hidden land, the mountains in the distance broke through, their rugged peaks blue, the hollows between filled with pockets of snow.

'Would you like to visit the huskies?' Eddie asked.

'I'd love to!'

'Well, we'll have to have permission for that. Seems they reckon it's bad for them to have too many visitors. Nat Mitchell, now, he's the man to see.'

But the dog-handler seemed to be elusive. No one had seen him about. They approached a group of men who were busy wiring one of the buildings to the ground, and Kerin was surprised to recognise Dain Ransome, with a mallet in his hand, driving steel spikes into the frozen earth.

He glanced up and seeing Eddie, handed him a piece of wire cable.

'Here,' he said. 'Get that secured, will you?' He walked a little further away to pick up another long spike, and Eddie, busy with the cable, asked, 'Have you seen Mitch?'

'Down with the dogs. Why?'

'I was going to take Kerin down to see them.'

'You're needed here.'

Eddie shrugged. 'Sorry, Kerin.'

'That's okay.' Dain Ransome had his back to her, positioning the spike. 'Can I help?' she asked.

He glanced up, mallet in hand. 'This isn't a job for—you,' he said briefly.

Holding her temper, she reminded him, 'You said there's no union demarcation here.'

He grasped the spike in a hard fist and tapped the head of it smartly.

Kerin persisted, 'I drive a mean nail.'

He glanced up at her and her heart thumped, just once. Because unbelievably, there was a hint of grudging laughter in the ice-blue of his eyes. He stopped what he was doing and really looked at her, taking in the fur-lined hood pushed back from a face bare of make-up, the hair pulled back and tied neatly at her nape, the sensible windproof trousers and clumsy mukluks. The mallet swung gently at his side, and he said, 'There's a man putting up shelves in the mess. Maybe he could use a lady nail-driver.'

She turned smartly and went back to the mess with a sense of triumph.

She didn't drive too many nails, but the man who was working in the mess, erecting bookshelves right along one wall, seemed pleased to have someone to hold pieces of timber and pass bits and pieces when he needed them. When she asked him, 'Will I do as a carpenter's apprentice?' he said, 'You'll do. I'll shout you a drink on the strength of it.'

He opened a door beside a pass-through with a roller closure that Kerin had assumed was the bar, looked back at her a little doubtfully, and said, 'Just hang on a minute.'

She waited, wondering, and then the screen rolled up and Fergus was saying, 'What'll you have, Kerin?'

She asked for gin and lime, and surveyed the array of bottles with some awe. It was undeniably a well-stocked bar. Fergus poured her drink and helped himself to a small whisky, leaning an elbow on the bar to drink it. His shirt buttons strained, and she saw a corner of white paper briefly protruding. Idly she ran her eyes along the bare wall above the bar. Presumably she had just been spared the sight of another example of erotic art.

He rinsed their glasses at the small sink and then closed up the hatch again. 'Officially, the bar doesn't open until after the evening meal,' he explained. 'But Dain's a reasonable man about that sort of thing. He doesn't come the heavy unless someone abuses privileges.'

'You've worked with him before?' Kerin asked.

'Once. Not the chummy sort, exactly, but a good man in a tight spot, and not the sort to stand by cracking the whip while everyone else does the donkey-work, either. We'll make out with him.'

Lunch was sausages and mashed potatoes followed by scones dripping with butter and two choices of jam. Kerin decided death from starvation was unlikely these days in the Antarctic. But of course, it wasn't starvation so much as scurvy, allied to the appalling conditions, that had plagued Robern Falcon Scott and his party on their epic journey to the Pole. Captain Cook had known back in the eighteenth century that fresh fruit would prevent scurvy, but that wasn't available to Scott, and the vital discovery that it was the vitamin C content that was the preventative agent was yet to be made.

After lunch she went back to helping her new partner, and even got to drive a few nails herself, proving that she was quite competent at it, too. She couldn't help hoping that Fergus might just happen to mention that some time, when he was talking to Dain Ransome.

They cleared up the mess when two other men came in to set the tables again, and after another hearty meal Kerin had a drink with Fergus and Les, watching with secret amusement the surprised looks passed at the empty space above the rows of bottles. She fancied her presence might be a little inhibiting to certain of the gentlemen present, and went off to her room to take out her portable type-writer and type up some of the notes she had taken during the day. Not that there were many. She had contented herself mainly with general impressions during the morning, and kept her notebook and pencil unobtrusively out of sight most of the time, wanting to give the men time to get used to her presence. Some people found notebooks or tape-recorders intimidating. Kerin had a recorder, but felt she should be cautious about its use.

She was surprised when she heard footsteps in the passageway outside her room, and even more so when a peremptory hand tapped on her door.

Expecting to see Eddie or perhaps Guy, she clutched at the edge of the door with slight shock when she saw the tall figure of Dain Ransome standing there instead.

His light eyes went past her to the paper in her type-writer. 'You're working?' he asked, almost too politely, for him.

'Yes,' she said, obscurely pleased that he hadn't caught her reading a book, although heaven knew it was well past working hours. 'But it can wait. Did you want me?'

His mouth moved in a way that should have made it smile, but the way his eyes flicked over her made it more of a derisive sneer. She was thankful she didn't blush easily.

He asked, 'Do you still want to see those dogs?'

'Yes.'

'I'll take you,' he said.

For a moment she was so surprised she could only look back at him blankly.

'Well?' he said impatiently. 'You don't need to change. Just put on a few more clothes.'

'Yes,' she said. 'Thank you. I won't be long.'

'There's no hurry,' he drawled as he leaned against the door-jamb, looking away from her down the passageway, while she hastily pulled on the cumbersome windproof gear. 'It won't be getting dark for six months or so.'

She laughed, a soft, vibrant sound in her throat that made him turn his head suddenly and look at her.

Her fingers fumbled with the zip of her parka, and he suddenly stepped into the room, making it seem very small, and took over, clipping in the fastening and pulling it up to her chin.

'Thank you,' she said steadily, and he stepped back, saying in an impersonal voice, 'Ready?'

'Yes, thank you.'

'You're very polite all of a sudden,' he observed mockingly as they moved into the passageway and he reached forward to open the first of the metal doors.

'*You're* very considerate all of a sudden,' Kerin retorted.

'My mother brought me up to open doors for ladies,' he said, and beat her to the next one as her fingers were about to close over the handle.

'Don't you regard that as a concession?' she asked, stepping out into the crisp coldness of the outside air.

'I regard it as a habit,' he returned. 'One that's hard to break.'

'Habits of mind are hard to break, too,' she said, cheerfully watching her feet, because she wasn't yet used to the clumsy boots, and the melting snow made the ground hazardous to walk. If she slipped it would be a choice between falling ignominiously at his feet or grabbing at him to save her. She didn't fancy either alternative.

He hadn't responded to her last remark, and she said, 'Some of them are just prejudice, when you get down to it.'

'Leave it, Kerin,' he said quite gently, and because his casual use of her name for the first time had given her an unexpected jolt, she did.

They were walking on cleaner snow now, hard-packed and slippery on the surface. They had to negotiate one of the pressure ridges that from a distance resembled frozen ocean breakers, but at close quarters seemed more like a strewn pile of huge ice-blocks. Dain Ransome didn't offer to help her, but she could see him keeping a sharp eye on her as they climbed over.

Then they were on the flat surface of the ice shelf, and

could see the dog lines. A bulky figure in a bright yellow parka waved at them, and Dain Ransome lifted a hand in acknowledgement. 'I told Mitch you were coming,' he said. 'He's ready to answer questions.'

Nat Mitchell was a stocky high-country shepherd, dark-eyed and with a respectable growth of curly black beard. His handclasp almost crushed Kerin's fingers even through the thick mittens they both wore, and a broad grin parted the beard as he said, 'I met Kerin yesterday, Dain.'

She counted eleven dogs, spaced apart on the lines, and she turned to Nat and asked, 'Is it true that they have to be kept apart because they're so prone to fighting?'

'Nope. That used to be what happened, but our huskies are tied so they can talk to the neighbours if they want to. You don't put them next to a dog they don't get along with. They do scrap a bit, in some circumstances, but like most dogs, their temperament depends a lot on how you treat them. The Arctic dogs' reputation for savagery was literally a case of giving a dog a bad name. At Scott the dogs are given the freedom of the base after a run, and they've never abused the privilege. They get on just fine with people.'

'Could I pat one?' Kerin asked, longing to get the feel of the shaggy, soft-looking fur.

The dog-handler cast a quick look at Dain Ransome, who returned one that she couldn't read, then Mitch said, 'Sure,' with a nonchalance that she felt hid something else. 'Come and meet Chinook,' he invited, and stopped in front of the nearest dog, which lifted a black muzzle in a sandy-gold face and made small, welcoming noises. 'Go ahead.'

He was grinning, and Kerin sensed some kind of trap. 'Is it all right to take off my glove?' she asked, stalling. But they wouldn't be stupid enough to let her get bitten. Even Dain Ransome wouldn't go that far.

'Sure,' said Mitch, still grinning.

Suspiciously, she looked at Dain Ransome again, but the blandness of his expression gave her no help, and she stripped off her mitten and glove from her right hand and let the dog sniff it, then stroked the beautiful head, as he nuzzled at her parka, his plumed tail waving.

'Oh, you lovely fellow!' she said, laughing and going down on her knee, then drawing back as a cold nose nudged her cheek. She straightened up and said, 'He's as gentle as a lamb! So much for the savage husky!'

'And now you can pat the rest of them,' said Dain Ransome.

It sounded like an order, and she looked at him curiously. Nat Mitchell laughed outright and said, 'That's the rule, Kerin. You pet one, you pet them all. One fault of the husky is his jealousy. Making a favourite of one is asking for trouble. It might not be until the next time out in the traces, but they'll vent their resentment on him eventually. Then you'd see how savage they *can* be. That's why we don't encourage people to visit the dogs at random. It can cause trouble.'

Kerin shrugged, laughing. So they had been having a small joke at her expense, but it wasn't a cruel one, and she didn't mind. She duly went all the way down the line and was introduced to the dogs in turn, making sure they all got equal treatment, and when she was finished, Dain Ransome said, 'Put your gloves on.'

She said, 'You bet!' cheerfully but with fervour, because her hand felt frozen, but just as she was fumbling with her glove, he shot out a hand and grabbed her wrist, saying, 'Let me see!'

The tips of two fingers were showing white, and he said, 'Why didn't you *say* you were that cold?' and unzipping his parka, pushed her hand inside it, under the warmth of the woollen shirt covering his hard chest. Apparently acclimatised, he wore no woollen undershirt.

She stood quietly, feeling the beat of his heart under her palm, and the warm palm of his mitten covering her hand under his clothes. *'Forget about old wives' tales such as putting snow on frostbite,'* they had said at the survival course. *'The best cure is body warmth—your own or your partner's.'*

He would have done the same thing for Nat or any of the men, she told herself firmly—only they wouldn't have felt the way she did, small tingles of awareness sensitising her skin as the warmth against her hand seemed to enter it and spread throughout her body.

Her fingers were tingling too, quite painfully, and she said, her voice quite steady, 'I think it's all right now, thank you.'

'Hurting?'

'Yes.'

'Good.' He stayed there a moment longer and then withdrew her hand, still held in his, and looked at it. 'Put your gloves on,' he repeated. 'We'd better get back.'

Nat said casually, 'Okay?'

'Fine,' said Kerin, turning to him with relief. 'My first taste of the kiss of the Antarctic.'

'Kiss or kill,' Dain Ransome said almost absently. 'It's all one to her.'

Mitch looked a bit puzzled as he fell into step beside them. But Kerin knew exactly what he meant.

When they got back to the base, Dain said, 'Come on, we'll have a drink in the mess.'

They left their windproofs in the porch and walked into a pleasantly warm fug of cigarette smoke and the sound of music and talk. Several of the men looked up and smiled at Kerin and as she sipped her drink at a table with the two men, Mitch with his elbows on the table and Dain Ransome leaning casually back, tipping his chair, she felt a warm glow of belonging. Even the ice-blue of Dain Ransome's eyes seemed to have thawed a little. Tonight he had been quite human.

Encouraged, she began asking him about the base, details of its purpose, design and construction. He replied with lazy tolerance and eventually asked, 'Can you remember all this?'

'Most of it,' she said. 'I do have a tape-recorder, though.

Would you object if I used it some time to interview you—as base commander?'

'No. Would you like to see the original plans and instructions for setting up the station?' he asked. 'They're in my office.'

'Could I? That would be great.'

He finished his drink and said, 'Come on then,' glancing at her empty glass. 'Unless you want another?'

She shook her head and got up. They picked up their windproofs but didn't put them on for the trek through the buildings to his office. He hung both lots of clothing up outside and ushered her in. She had to admit his mother had trained him well. Fervent supporter of women's rights though she was, she couldn't help feeling a vague regret that they seemed to spell the end of old-fashioned courtesy. A pity *that* sort of virtue seemed to go with male chauvinism of the worst kind.

'Sit down while I find it,' he said, turning to look along the shelves.

She didn't like to appropriate the chair, perching on the edge of the desk instead, and looking about the businesslike little room, noting the complete absence of any personal note. Apart from her own quarters it must be about the only room that didn't have either a wife-and-family photo or a pin-up. She wondered what his bedroom was like.

He had turned, a file in his hand, and was watching her.

'Looking for something?' he asked.

'Pin-ups,' she said. 'I suppose you keep yours in your own room.' And she supposed she shouldn't have said that, but they had been almost friends, these last couple of hours. And friends could say these things.

An unreadable gleam had entered his eyes. He said, 'I don't require that kind of stimulus.'

She wasn't sure what he meant by that, but recalling Eddie's solemn theory, she smiled irresistibly. Obviously, *that* wasn't Dain Ransome's reason. If anyone was, he was all man.

'Something funny?' he enquired.

Her eyes full of laughter, she looked up at him as he stepped closer. 'Just a theory of Eddie's,' she said lightly.

He stopped only a foot away. The gleam in his eyes had intensified, and with dismay she saw that it held anger and something just as devastating and even more frightening. 'I know all about Eddie's theories!' he snapped, and threw the file on to the desk beside her. Then his hands closed on her shoulders and he jerked her off her perch and into his arms.

For a few seconds she was plain terrified, resisting him with all her strength. He simply tightened his hold until it hurt, and his mouth bruised hers. Even through the thickness of her jersey she felt the grip of his hands, the warmth of the body that pressed itself ruthlessly against the length of hers.

With a choked, protesting sound in her throat, she gave up the unequal fight and prepared to endure the punishment. And then suddenly it wasn't punishment any longer. Dain still held her tightly, but his hands on her back were caressing, not hurtful, and his mouth began a sensuous coaxing movement on hers that gradually made her relax against him and obediently open her lips until he sent her spinning into an other-world of mindless, breathless sensation.

Time spun away between them, and she wanted the kiss to endure for ever, but he slowly broke it off, bringing her back to earth, and then moved away, still holding her shoulders, his thumbs caressing them as she dropped her head, afraid to let him see what was in her eyes.

Then his hands dropped, and he said, mockery in his voice that set her quivering, 'Maybe that will set your mind at rest, regarding Eddie's theories.'

He moved, and she instinctively flinched, but he only picked up the file and thrust it into her hands. 'Bring that back when you've finished with it,' he said impersonally.

Kerin risked one look at his face as her fingers closed on the cardboard cover. It seemed expressionless, except for a slightly ironic look in his eyes that she couldn't bear.

Trying to match it, she said, 'Thanks. I'm sure I'll find this instructive—too,' and left the room with her head high.

CHAPTER SIX

KERIN spent the following morning reading that file and making notes. Every now and then the words blurred as she found her mind wandering and reverting to those few incredible minutes when Dain Ransome, the man of ice, had suddenly become almost too human.

But it hadn't been the result of genuine feeling, just a calculated punishment for what he apparently saw as her daring to laugh at his expense.

Beast! she thought, and forced herself to concentrate on the words she was trying to read.

She handed the file back to him at lunch, because she didn't want to go to his office again. She thanked him coolly, returning his slightly mocking glance with a calculatedly indifferent one of her own.

She went and sat with Sebastian Wright and another biologist, who were talking about a penguin rookery they hoped to study. Sebastian had unruly fair hair that hung in curls over his forehead, and had apparently decided to follow the prevailing fashion of the Antarctic and grow a beard. His chin was covered with a fine gold stubble. The other man, an earlier arrival, already sported about an inch of downy growth.

Kerin listened with interest to their conversation, her back to Dain's table, but half-way through the meal discovered herself wondering why two men with such similar colouring as Dain and Sebastian should look so utterly different, and comparing Dain's cool stare with the eager light in Sebastian's blue eyes. The biologist would be easily ten years younger, but she didn't think it was a matter of age alone.

A chair scraped back, and without looking round she knew that Dain had left the room. Immediately some tension within her unwound, and she was able to laugh naturally at some joke Sebastian made, and relax with the men over their coffee.

Later she put film into her camera and wandered about outside, taking pictures of the views and the activity about the base.

There was no wind, and most of the men worked bare-headed and with shirtsleeves rolled up, in balmy sunlight, but anywhere the shade fell from the buildings one was immediately conscious that the temperature hovered about freezing point.

Among a group of men heaving up a prefabricated wall Kerin caught a glimpse of fair hair glinting in the sun, a dark plaid shirt covering broad shoulders, and narrow hips in blue jeans. Hastily she turned away, but a moment later he must have spotted her, and called her name.

Reluctantly she turned and he strode over to her, his eyes flicking to the camera and then back to her face.

'Busy?' he asked.

'Just taking some preliminary snaps,' she said. 'Catching the end of the first stage of a new station.'

'When you've finished,' he said, 'there's a job you might do.'

'Now,' she said, 'if you like.'

A faint smile on his lips, he remarked, 'Willing, aren't you?' and she didn't know if he meant that to have a double meaning.

'I aim to please, Commander,' she told him calmly, well aware that she was here under sufferance.

The smile hardened as he said, 'I'm sure you will.' His eyes swept over her unfastened parka over a shapeless thick jersey and her green wool pants as though he had no trouble visualising what was underneath them. He wasn't going to let her forget her sex.

Then he said, 'We have some boxes of books to go on some of those shelves you helped Fergus with yesterday. I've got one of the men to put them in the mess room.

Think you could sort them out and put them out on the shelves?'

'I suppose so. Any particular order?'

He shrugged. 'Whatever seems best to you. It seems a suitable job for an Information Officer.'

Kerin supposed it was, and wondered if he had stressed it to prove he hadn't asked her simply because she was a woman and to be spared the heavier tasks. But he had said she wasn't to expect special treatment.

She didn't know if it had been a concession to get one of the men to bring in the boxes, but when she saw them she was glad that he had. She would have managed somehow, but the boxes were heavy and she didn't relish the thought of having to carry them.

There was quite a library, including books about the Antarctic itself, some best-sellers, a few classics, biographies, some craft books, some others on a wide variety of subjects, and a selection of paperbacks which seemed to be mainly of the blood-and-blondes variety.

Kerin sorted them roughly into categories and arranged them neatly on the new shelves. She had brought a few books along herself, and she supposed most of the men would have some, too. With these, and a general sharing among themselves, they shouldn't run short of reading matter for some time.

She didn't see Ransome again until the evening meal. She had changed into a pair of jeans herself, beginning to feel acclimatised, and teamed them with a light wool jersey that gently skimmed her figure instead of enveloping it. At the last minute she put on Roger's ring.

A few of the men cast her appreciative glances, and Eddie hailed her with a cheerful grin and a soft whistle. Eddie would have any ardent Women's Libber tearing her hair with rage, Kerin had no doubt, but he was harmless and didn't mean anything by it.

She got a tray of food and found Dain at her elbow. 'Sit with me,' he said. 'I want to talk to you.'

She supposed that was an order, so she shrugged and accompanied him to a corner table which they had to themselves.

She put her plate on the table, sat down and lifted a knife and fork, facing Dain across the gay plastic flowers printed on the tablecloth, and said, 'Well?'

He lifted expressionless eyes from her left hand and said, 'Eat first.'

She did, quite well, less from hunger than from a determination not to let him think he could affect her healthy appetite. It was steak and vegetables with a delicious rich gravy, followed by apple pie and tinned cream, and Dain did full justice to it, too.

Over their coffee, against a subdued buzz of talk from the other tables, he said, 'Scott Base sent a bag of mail over on the plane with your lot, that got dropped off there weeks ago, and somehow missed the last run out of Hillary. I've just got round to reading it. There was a letter from the Superintendent, Antarctic Division—mostly about you.'

Kerin cradled her coffee cup in her two hands and looked up into an impersonal blue gaze.

'So,' she said carefully, 'now you know.'

'Yes, now I know. You are a spy after all.'

Her soft lips firmed and she put down the cup without drinking from it. She kept her voice low, but it shook a little with anger. 'That isn't fair!'

He picked up his own cup and drank from it, then replaced it in its saucer before he replied. Surprisingly, he said, levelly, 'Okay, maybe it wasn't. You're a "psychological observer", then. Is there much difference?'

'Of course there's a difference! Professor Prince wants the men's reactions reported, but naturally he doesn't want them to know they're being observed because their behaviour wouldn't be natural, then. It wouldn't give a typical picture at all.'

'A typical picture is what he wants?'

'Yes, of course.'

'But if the men knew you were reporting on their reactions to the environment, that would be introducing an alien factor that might distort the results of the study, right?'

'Yes, exactly.' She looked up at him almost eagerly. He was a scientist, he understood. She could understand his initial reaction—she hadn't liked the idea a bit, herself, at first.

But he was studying her with faint derision in his green eyes, in the slight curve of his mouth. 'Good God!' he exclaimed. 'Is the man out of his cotton-picking mind?'

Kerin blinked and said coldly, 'He has a mind that could probably run rings around yours,' although that wasn't true. Dain Ransome was no fool, and in his own field was at least as well respected as Professor Prince in his.

'I've no doubt,' Dain rejoined. 'But he knows damn all about men in the Antarctic.'

'He's been studying them for years!'

'Well, he hasn't learned much!'

'He knows there are gaps in the data. That's why he wants me to help.'

'*You!*'

'I happen to be a trained psychologist,' she informed him with cold calm. 'Didn't the letter say that?'

But he brushed that aside with a short, derisory laugh. 'What *you* are,' he said with deliberation, 'is an alien factor. One woman in a bunch of men. What the Professor should have realised is that your presence will screw up his precious data more thoroughly than a daily announcement that our every move is being psychoanalysed by an appointed board of experts.'

'That's ridiculous!'

'Is it? Already three men who were growing beards have shaved them off. The theory is women don't go for beards. Although there was some difference of opinion. One or two are convinced that a bit of facial adornment turns a woman on. Someone even suggested asking you, but they got shy. They don't feel they know you well enough, yet.'

'You're making this up,' she said stubbornly.

He held her eyes with his, long enough to show her he

didn't like the implication that he was lying. Then he said flatly, 'No.'

'Well, when they do know me,' she said defiantly, 'they'll know it doesn't matter. I'll be just one of the team, like everyone else.'

'Just one of the boys?' he said ironically. 'Not you.'

'Why not me?' she demanded. 'I'm not the first woman in the Antarctic, by a long chalk. Some of the men must have worked with women here before——'

'They didn't look like you.'

For a minute she floundered, taken by surprise. Then she said, 'If that was meant to be a compliment——'

'It wasn't.'

'Then I won't thank you for it!'

Dain raised an eyebrow and inclined his blond head in a travesty of politeness, and she wanted to hit him.

'Anyway,' she went on, trying to recollect her train of thought, 'most of them must have worked with women at some time. It's not *so* different here——' He interrupted there with a small, derisive crack of laughter, and she went on, simmering with contained rage, 'And it's your own fault I'm the only woman here. *You* stopped Rose Carson from coming!'

'I didn't say so,' he reminded her.

No, he wouldn't. He was too clever to give her an admission that she might use against him.

'You didn't need to,' she retorted. 'I know how your mind works!'

He was laughing at her again, but silently this time. 'Really? That must be interesting!'

'No, it isn't!' she said smartly. 'It's so predictable!'

'Well, that's one thing that couldn't be said of you—or any woman.'

Scornfully she said, 'How you do generalise! Remarks like that arise from sheer prejudice.'

'Or experience.'

She didn't want to get into a discussion of his experience of women. He certainly had some, if that kiss had been anything to go by. Apart from the initial violence, his technique had been wellnigh faultless.

Unknowingly, her gaze had slipped to his firmly sculpted mouth, and to cover her thoughts she said, '*You* don't wear a beard.'

'No. Perhaps I should have told them that you don't require a beard to turn you on.'

Too late, Kerin realised she had left herself wide open for that. Dain Ransome didn't fight fair.

Before she could think of an adequate comeback he spoke again, his voice sounding quite impersonal, as though they were discussing the weather. 'Is the ring a keep-off-the-grass sign?'

Flatly, she said, 'It's an engagement ring.'

After a moment's silence, he said, 'You weren't wearing it last night.'

Did that mean he wouldn't have kissed her if she had been? Somehow she doubted it would have made a scrap of difference.

'It doesn't go under gloves,' she explained.

'You weren't wearing it last time I saw you, either.'

'Last time?' He had hardly glanced at her that night, had shown no sign of recognising her at all.

'At that restaurant in Christchurch. You saw me,' he said calmly.

'That was the night Roger asked me to marry him. I wasn't taking much notice of anyone else.'

'Naturally.' She couldn't read the expression on his face.

'Right there in the restaurant, actually,' she told him, driven by some obscure instinct. *While you watched, and I hardly even heard him,* she remembered, with sudden shock.

'By candlelight,' Dain drawled. 'How romantic!' His face hadn't changed, but there was a deep spark in his eyes that looked like anger.

'Yes, it was,' Kerin agreed, a little breathless, because that deep anger rather frightened her, although she would have died rather than admit it.

'So Roger's the lucky man. The poor trusting fool doesn't know you, does he?'

Fury brought her to her feet, pushing back her chair with such force that it rocked. Blindly she turned away from the table and made for the door, catching a brief glimpse of surprise and curiosity on the faces of the men at the next table. She glanced back as she manipulated the heavy door-handle and saw Dain still sitting where she had left him, his hand gently holding his coffee cup, his face a cold, indifferent mask.

Through the cold passageways between the buildings, she hardly felt the chill, anger driving her feet at speed along the wet boards, and generating warmth of its own.

She hurried into her own room and slammed the door behind her, then stood against it, hugging her arms about her while she called Dain Ransome a few choice names under her breath. She would have liked to go out for a long, long walk, but she didn't feel like company, and there wasn't anywhere she could go alone.

Well, she could work, and maybe forget him and his offensive remarks in that.

She got out some paper and rolled it into the typewriter, and made three mistakes in the first line. She ripped out the paper, screwed it savagely into a tight ball, and threw it into a corner of the room. Which was silly, of course. There was a minute wastebasket under the table where the typewriter stood, and sooner or later she would have to pick up the ball of paper and dispose of it properly.

Well—later, then. She took another piece of paper and slid a carbon and copy sheet under it, and typed a line very slowly.

Five minutes later the door opened, and she turned from the typewriter as Dain Ransome came in and shut it behind him.

'Don't you ever knock?' she demanded furiously, getting to her feet.

'I did last night,' he reminded her. 'Not this time.'

'I might have been——'

'Undressed?' he asked mockingly. 'Hardly. You were banging away at that machine so hard you wouldn't have heard me anyway.'

'Do you usually barge into people's rooms uninvited?'

'Only yours. I didn't think you'd invite me.'

'You're damn right I wouldn't! And you can just——'

'*Shut up!* I'll say what I came to say and then I'll go. Don't you ever do that to me again, Kerin.'

'What?'

'I said, *don't* you walk out on me in a paddy again. I won't have it.'

Furious, she took a deep breath and asked in a shaking voice, 'Is that an order, Commander?'

'If that's what you want to call it. I'm responsible for the morale of this station, and that won't be enhanced by the sight of the Information Officer scrapping with me in public.'

'I might remind you, Commander, I wasn't "scrapping", as you call it. I walked out because if I stayed another minute I would have been tempted to throw my cup at you. And that would really have given the men something to think about!'

'And me?' She was sure that twitch at his mouth couldn't be a smile.

'*And* you!'

'I'd advise you not to try it,' he said quietly, but she wasn't deceived by the tone. He meant he could rip her apart if she tried.

'Is that a threat?' she asked defiantly.

'That's advice. And you'd better take it.'

'I might—if *you*'ll take some from me.'

His eyes narrowed a little, and he said, 'That depends.'

'If I were you,' she said, 'I'd refrain from making insulting remarks, unless you're prepared for some retaliation.'

'Point taken,' he said after a moment. 'But don't expect an apology for what I said.'

'Why did you say it?' she demanded. 'Because of—last night?'

'How did you guess?' he mocked her.

Kerin bit her lip. 'Is it any use reminding you that you didn't give me much choice?' she asked in a low voice.

'At first, perhaps,' he acknowledged. 'But you didn't put up much of a fight.'

She supposed she hadn't, really. There had come a point when it seemed silly to resist, mostly because she didn't really want to.

'You'd better go,' she said coldly.

'In a minute. Believe me, I'm no more anxious for your company than you are for mine. Unfortunately, unless you change your mind within the next few days, we're stuck with each other. I'll make a bargain with you. You don't cause trouble among the men, and I'll do all I can to make your job easy.'

'You're paranoid!' she exclaimed, staring. 'I'm making no promises and no bargains, Mr Ransome. I'll do my job, with or without your gracious help. And I'll do it well!'

His cold eyes glittered at her. 'Just so long as you stick to your job,' he said. 'And save the rest for Roger.'

Kerin was so angry she felt herself shaking with it, and clenched her fingers to stop the trembling. 'You are the most offensive man I've ever met!' she told him. 'You did say you were going.'

'So I did.' But he stayed looking at her flushed face and furiously bright eyes a few moments longer, seeming to find them amusing.

'You'd like to hit me, wouldn't you?' he said softly.

Even her voice shook with the rage that consumed her. 'Very much!'

'Then I'll give you an excuse,' he said, suddenly stepping closer.

He took her completely by surprise, cupping her chin in a hard hand while his mouth descended on hers in a brief, hurtful, contemptuous kiss.

Her hand flew up as he lifted his head, but he was prepared for it, of course, catching her wrist, and then the other one, in a painfully tight grasp, his mouth parting in a wolfish grin as he watched her impotent efforts to free herself.

It wasn't doing any good, and she stopped and stood taut and angry, her eyes blazing hatred into his.

'Well, you really tried that time,' he taunted her. 'Roger would have been proud of you.'

Kerin didn't answer him, her breath coming hard and fast, her head thrown back defiantly, every muscle straining against that implacable hold on her wrists. He was hurting her, but she wouldn't whimper, she wouldn't beg. Not to him.

Then quite suddenly he let her go, and she stepped back to put her hands behind her and clutch at the support of the table.

His glance flickered over her, and his mouth seemed to tighten. Then he turned away and at last left the room, closing the door quite gently behind him.

CHAPTER SEVEN

THE spring drew on, and life settled into something resembling a routine. The population at the base was depleted as field parties were flown into the mountains of Marie Byrd Land for geological studies of the exposed rock at their peaks, and three men went with the dog team across the ice shelf to set up a small weather station. Other parties were ferried from the base by helicopter each day and returned to its home comforts in time for dinner.

The days, of course, were regulated strictly by the clock, for as the season progressed, the sun simply wheeled around the horizon, then settled into a steady glow day and night, and sunset and sunrise came together, casting an eerie glow of midnight blue and brilliant gold across the snow.

Nobody worked strictly regular hours, but some sort of daily routine of sleep and work and leisure was maintained, both for the sake of mental and physical health and for the maintenance of work schedules and general management of the station.

Kerin took her turn as a 'house mouse' like all the men, cleaning the mess and setting tables, washing dishes and helping the cook. The men vetoed her cleaning their ablutions block, though, leaving her responsible for her own small bathroom.

She went out on the water collection run, learning how to drive the motorised toboggan that the men called a 'tin dog' as opposed to the huskies which were labelled 'shaggy dogs'. The water for the base was melted from big blocks of ice cut from the pressure ridges, and transported back to the big ice-melter at the base on a sled behind the 'tin dog'.

As much as it was possible in a small and close-living community, Kerin kept out of Dain's way, and when he

85

had to speak to her he did so with cool, authoritative courtesy.

He stopped by her table at breakfast one morning and said, 'We're having visitors for a couple of days—four American Senators. Think you could show them about?'

'Yes. When do they arrive?'

'Tomorrow. We'd better both meet the plane. About ten, I believe.'

One of the Senators turned out to be a woman, a fact which, Kerin noted sourly, Dain took in his stride. Not only that, he gave the Senator a smile of considerable charm and made sure she got the front seat in the sno-cat that transported them to the base. He carried the woman's bags himself to the room beside Kerin's and gave her another of his incredible smiles before assuring her that Kerin would look after her.

Kerin did, of course, finding it perfectly easy because Belle Yates was friendly and energetic and very willing to be pleased. She had a pleasantly pretty face and a slightly plump figure, and would have been about fiftyish. 'A bit old to be tramping round the Antarctic, I guess,' she said frankly. 'But what the hell, you only live once, and the chance was there, so I took it. Of course, we're only tourists, really, not like you young folks—you and that nice Mr Ransome.'

She ate at Dain's table that night, and it turned out to be almost a party. There was champagne and the cook had opened up some of the luxury goods usually kept for later in the season, in honour of the guests. Oysters and asparagus spears figured on the menu, and the ice cream that followed the carpet-bag steaks was decorated with rounds of kiwi-fruit that sent the visitors into raptures.

Belle sat at Dain's right hand, and Kerin, at the other end of the table, watched him being almost gallant to the older woman, with increasing irritation. Once he looked across and found her looking at him, and raised an eyebrow enquiringly. Kerin turned away and bestowed a brilliant smile on the middle-aged congressman at her side, who was asking if she had been to the Pole.

'No, I haven't,' she said regretfully. 'I may get the chance if I'm lucky, but lots of people who work in the Antarctic never do get to see the actual South Pole itself.'

'Hey, now! That's a shame,' the Senator said.

'Oh, it doesn't matter,' Kerin smiled. 'Getting this far is quite something.'

'I guess you're right,' he agreed, but later when the tables were cleared and they were sitting about in the comfort of the armchairs and sofas grouped at one end of the room, she was sitting in between him and Belle, and he leaned across her and said earnestly to the other woman, 'Did you know that some people actually working here never get to the South Pole? Kerin here tells me she might have to go home without even seeing it.'

'Why, what a shame!' exclaimed Belle, echoing her colleague's words. 'Now me, I wouldn't go home without seeing it! That's our next stop, you know, dear, after we leave Hillary. The Pole, and then back to McMurdo Sound, and home. Well, it's short, but it's been the trip of a lifetime.'

She was sure it was, Kerin was saying, when Eddie Priest came up looking a little diffident, asking for a word with Senator Yates.

'Some of us was wondering, ma'am,' he said ultra-politely, 'if you would care to dance a little. It isn't often we have two ladies present, you see, and—well, we'd be honoured, if you and Kerin don't mind——'

'A dance? Why, Mr Priest, that's a wonderful idea!' Belle told him, beaming.

Glancing at Ransome, Kerin somehow thought he didn't agree, but the men were already moving tables and someone was putting a record on the turntable of the stereo system in one corner of the room. Belle did a sedate foxtrot with Eddie, and the other Senator claimed Kerin for the first dance. After that they were both kept on the floor, the men having a thoroughly enjoyable time, and those who had claimed one dance already hanging back to allow others a fair turn.

When Kerin had danced briefly with almost everyone but the guests and Dain Ransome, and the music had been gradually getting livelier and the dances more strenuous, someone put on, at Belle's laughing request, a slow number. Kerin saw Guy Halsey, whose good-looking, bony face still remained unshaven, and Sebastian Wright, the blond-bearded biologist, converging on her.

She had a glimpse of a few sly grins and expectant looks on the faces of the men about the room as they reached her together, and then a hard hand encircled her waist, and Dain's voice said, 'My dance, I think, Kerin.'

He swept her into the centre of the floor, leaving the two young men with identical expressions of surprised chagrin, staring after them, and she couldn't help a small laugh. Judging from the expressions on some of the other faces that she could see, she wasn't the only one who was amused, either.

The hand on her back tightened, hard fingers almost crushed hers in them. 'Does it amuse you?' he asked glacially.

Cautiously she said, 'What do you mean?'

'Playing off one man against another. Which would you have chosen?'

'I don't know,' she said, trying to keep calm. 'Actually, you're the one playing games. Why did you ask me to dance?'

'Why not? You've danced with everyone else.'

'*They* asked me because they wanted to dance with me.'

'They asked you because they wanted an excuse to hold you in their arms. Why should my reason be any different?'

For a moment she stopped dancing, but he nipped her waist with his fingers and gritted, 'Don't you make a scene here, Kerin, or I'll really make you sorry!'

Stiffly she moved her feet to his lead, muttering in a low, furious voice, 'You really go out of your way to be unpleasant, don't you?'

'As you go out of your way to be provocative.'

'I do nothing of the kind!' she protested.

He looked down at her, his mouth curving, and said, 'Perhaps that's an exaggeration. Does it just come naturally?'

She drew an impatient breath, and he said, 'Smile, Kerin. We're being watched.'

She flashed him a brilliant smile and snapped, 'Go to hell, Mr Ransome!'

To her surprise, the quality of his own smile changed, then, as though he was genuinely amused. 'Dain would be more friendly,' he suggested. 'And you're a lousy dancer —stiff as a poker.'

She stiffened even more at that and said, 'Actually, I'm quite a good dancer. With anyone else.'

'Do I make you nervous?'

'You make me furious!'

He threw back his head and laughed, whirling her about suddenly in a breathtaking couple of turns, and she automatically followed his lead. He looked down at her, saying, 'That's better, you're beginning to relax. You could be a good dancer, at that.'

Determined to show him how good she could be, Kerin made her body relax in his hold, and fluidly followed his lead. They actually danced well together, and she began to enjoy herself.

When the music came to an end, Dain kept his arm about her and led her back to where the guests were sitting, calling casually to the man at the turntable, 'Okay, Gus, that's enough for tonight.'

To the Senators, he said, smiling, 'You have an early start tomorrow. We're hoping to show you some seals. Think you can be up at six?'

'If we go to bed now,' said Belle, taking the hint. 'It's been a great party, Dain. You folks sure know how to enjoy yourselves, don't you?'

'Simple pleasures, Belle,' Dain smiled casually.

'Yes, indeed,' the Senator murmured. But as she and Kerin made their way to their own hut, Belle chuckled, and said, 'Your commander is a very smart man, isn't he?'

'He's a brilliant geologist.'

'Oh, I'm sure. But I was thinking more of his gift for handling people. I imagine he's also a brilliant strategist.'

'Why do you say that?'

'My dear, he just sent four United States Senators off to bed without a murmur of protest. And quite brilliantly prevented a possible problem from developing over you.'

'Me?' queried Kerin.

'Of course. One of those young men—the dark one— had obviously had rather a lot to drink. You might have found yourself a little embarrassed if Dain hadn't stepped in so smartly and asked you to dance himself. And then he made sure the party broke up immediately afterwards, without in the least seeming to exert any undue authority.'

'I'd have handled Guy,' Kerin assured her.

'Perhaps. But there might have been some element of resentment afterwards, and I imagine that could lead to trouble, in the rather unique conditions you people live in, here.'

And Dain couldn't risk that, of course, Kerin thought, as Belle bade her a cheerful goodnight. He wouldn't have danced with her at all if it hadn't been a tactical necessity.

The seals were found some way along the coast, a couple of hours journey by sno-cat. They trundled across the pressure ridges, noses lifting and dipping, and then negotiating the windblown ripples of snow called sastrugi, on to the snow-covered permanent ice shelf and then to the sea ice, ten feet thick over the Antarctic ocean itself.

Then they left the vehicles and walked with great care towards the sea's edge. The white was dazzling, even with sunglasses, and Kerin, trudging between Belle and Dain Ransome, was fascinated by the different shades and textures of an all-white world. There was the matt smoothness of the snow, the blue-white translucence of ice cliffs rearing up where icebergs had broken off and gone floating out to sea, the greenish tinge of floating ice as it moved lazily across the dark water of the bay, and the hard glassy glitter of thick ice beneath their feet as they walked across to investigate a breathing hole made by one of the seals.

There were a couple of them lying on the edge of the ice shelf like giant blackish-grey slugs, which lurched and toppled into the water at the approach of the strangers. A large flat-topped ice floe nudging the ice-shelf held twenty or so, some with babies, dark eyes blinking from a covering of downy white fur.

'Over there,' said Dain, pointing, and Belle lifted a pair of binoculars and gave an exclamation of satisfaction. Kerin could see a group of dark shapes gathered on the snow a little way inshore.

'We could walk over there,' Dain said.

'Oh, please!' Belle begged enthusiastically.

They approached from the sea side, cutting off the seals' retreat. Dain and one of the other men carried rifles, but the seals merely lifted their heads, waving them about a bit, and two or three flippered themselves across the ice and disappeared with a flick of their tails into holes gnawed in it. As they got closer there was some milling about, a couple of cries like barking, mingled with the sheep-like calls of the newborn pups.

The Americans were delighted, busily snapping pictures, and Kerin got a lovely close-up of one of the pups, inquisitively lifting its black nose at the intruders.

Then Dain called them away. 'That's enough disturbance,' he said. 'We don't want to frighten them, and disrupt their behaviour pattern. If they get upset it could endanger the pups and affect the breeding.'

Obediently they retired, and soon the group settled down and returned to its former somnolence.

As they moved back towards the machines there was a distant rumbling and crackling, like thunder, repeated at intervals. 'The ice is calving,' Dain explained. 'That's the sound of the thawing and breaking off process when the big bergs break away from the main mass of ice.'

As he spoke they approached a small mountain of rough-edged ice, diamond-bright icicles clinging and dripping from its jagged peaks, bathed in sapphire-blue light as the weak sun shone through it. 'That one,' Dain told them, 'didn't make it last year. It was floating out to sea when the sea froze again and trapped it for another season.'

'It's beautiful!' Kerin said softly.

Dain looked at her, as she pushed back her dark glasses to see the iceberg properly, and lifted her head in its fur-edged hood.

'Will it make it this season?' Belle asked.

'Maybe.' Dain took his eyes away from Kerin and looked up himself at the icy monster. 'When the ice lets go it'll be free—to float out to sea, maybe as far as New Zealand. But all the time it will be melting, losing its heart, until there's nothing left of it, and in the end warmth will destroy it. Warmth and softness and tropical comfort are the destroyers to the things of this place.'

'You make it sound sad,' said Belle, and Kerin moved her gaze from the trapped giant of ice and looked instead at Dain.

'*How much better this has all been,*' she said softly, '*than lounging in too great comfort at home!*'

'Is that a quotation?' Belle asked, puzzled.

'Robert Falcon Scott,' said Dain slowly, his eyes on Kerin's face. 'Written in the last stages of his return from the Pole, when he'd been beaten to it by Amundsen, had lost most of his men, and knew he was dying and would never see home again.'

'Well!' Belle said inadequately, looking from one to the other of them, in some perplexity. 'Well, I must say, you two understand each other very well!'

Kerin saw her own shock of surprise and rejection briefly mirrored in Dain's eyes before he turned away and looked at Belle, smiling. 'I wouldn't say that,' he said. 'I don't pretend to understand any woman, certainly not one like Kerin.'

Belle smiled back a little archly, and Kerin said, 'We'd better catch up with the others. They're leaving us behind.'

They parked the sno-tracks for a while a little further on,

and watched seals swimming gracefully between the flat-topped floes in the bay, leaping on to them from the water and lowering themselves clumsily back again.

Then there seemed to be a sudden flurry of activity, seals leaping, struggling and flopping on to the ice, and dark heads waving in agitation. Dain gripped Kerin's shoulder and pointed out to sea, then turned to the visitors and showed them where to look for the cause.

They were beautiful, two huge black and white, sleek shapes, arrowing smoothly through the water, scattering the floating, bobbing bits of melting ice, diving under the floes and weaving swiftly about the bigger bergs. Black dorsal fins cleaved a narrow path in the freezing water, and then a great black-topped head with white underjaw reared from the water and a row of saw-edged teeth threatened a baby seal only inches from the edge of the ice.

Kerin drew in a quick breath, Belle muffled a small scream with her mitten, and one of the men said in awed tones, '*What* the Jehosaphat *is* that?'

'Killer whales,' Dain told her. 'They come down here in spring to breed.'

For perhaps twenty minutes the whales cruised about the bay, while the seals huddled in apparent apprehension. One whale disappeared under one of the smaller ice floes holding three seals, and the watchers saw the shudder of the precarious raft as the great creature attacked from beneath, trying to dislodge the stubborn passengers. Three times the floe shook dangerously, but the ice was thick and strong, and the seals, nervously huddled together in the centre of it, escaped the sudden death that awaited them only inches from the safety of their precarious perch.

Eventually, foiled, the killers turned together and headed back to sea, in perfect unison, even executing a beautifully graceful, curving half-leap together before they disappeared, diving under with hardly a ripple.

'Wow!' exclaimed one of the men, lowering the cine camera he had been using. 'Wait'll I show them this back home. Boy, that was fantastic!'

'It sure was, Albie!' Belle agreed, and the other two men, as well as their driver, chorused assent.

Kerin said nothing, hugging to herself the excitement and awe of those unforgettable minutes, the memory of the terrible beauty of the killers, their deadly speed and grace, the power and purpose behind their silent, seeking and incredibly beautiful movements in the icy water.

Dain was silent, too, and she looked up and found his eyes on her, holding a question. And when she looked at him, the look in them changed. It said, *you, too.* She knew that what she had felt, he had shared, and she thought with a faint shock, *Belle was right. We do understand each other.* At least in some ways, it was true.

They were back at the base in time for lunch, and afterwards the visitors were taken on a short visit to one of the geological teams camped in the mountains, by helicopter.

During the afternoon the meteorologists arrived back with their dog team, and at the evening meal there was a great deal of hilarity at their table, attracting the attention of the whole room. Other men strolled over to the group, heads were bent, then guffaws of laughter followed.

Nat Mitchell came over to speak to Dain. 'Think we could use the hospital room for a while, Dain?' he asked. 'One of the dogs they brought back has a pretty nasty cut and I think it would be best if we could stitch it. Will you help?'

'Sure. What happened?'

'Some of the dogs got in a bit of a scrap on the way home. The mets had a bit of a job with them.'

'Is that the joke?' Dain asked mildly, his gaze on the men in question.

Nat gave a slightly embarrassed grin, glancing quickly at Belle and then Kerin. 'Sort of,' he said. 'I'll explain later.'

'I think,' Belle murmured to Kerin, leaning across the table, 'our feelings are being spared.'

Very likely, Kerin thought, smiling back. Curious, she wondered why.

Dain and Mitch were arranging to have the injured dog brought to the hospital room, and as Dain's chair scraped back Kerin leaned forward and asked, 'May I watch?'

Dain stood up, and even though she followed suit, she still looked up to him. 'It won't be nice,' he warned.

'I don't expect it will,' she retorted hardily. 'But as Information Officer, I'm interested.'

She thought his eyes hardened a little, then he shrugged. 'Okay. But if you faint, fall backwards.'

'I won't faint.'

He was turning away, but over his shoulder he looked back at her, his eyes slipping over her slimness in slacks and a fine wool jersey. She thought a smile tugged at his mouth before he turned away again, saying, 'Half an hour.'

She went to get her camera, looking back briefly at the door to see Dain bending his blond head to Albie—Senator Albert E. Marsh, she reminded herself, as the man, a fat cigar in one hand, plucked at the commander's sleeve with the other.

When she entered the small bare hospital room, the dog was already on the steel table, Mitch holding his head and talking to him while Dain slid a hypodermic needle into the animal's shoulder, eliciting nothing more than a small, surprised whimper.

Mitch went on murmuring soothing words in the dog's ear, and Dain pushed the plunger, removed the needle and glanced briefly round at Kerin, standing two steps inside the door.

'You can come closer,' he said. 'But don't get in the way.'

The dog gradually settled its head on its paws, gazing trustingly at Mitch, then eventually closed its dark eyes.

Already Dain was clipping with a pair of gleaming scissors at the matted hair about the wound. He finished the job with a razor.

'May I use a flash?' Kerin asked quietly.

Not lifting his head from the task, Dain said, 'Okay.'

When he had thoroughly cleaned the wound with swabs and picked up the needle and fine catgut thread, Mitch said jokingly, 'Maybe we should ask Kerin to do that.'

'The commander looks quite expert,' she said hastily. 'Are you trained, Mr Ransome?'

'I've learned the rudiments,' he said. 'But I'm no doctor. Stitching, injections and setting simple fractures is about my limit. It helps.'

She had taken two pictures already, and as he tied off the finished job she took another. Dain put down the needle on a stainless steel dish, laid his hand for a moment on the unconscious dog's head and said, 'I guess the patient will live.'

'I'll stay with him,' said Mitch, and Dain turned to wash his hands. As Kerin made to leave, he stopped her.

'Will you come to my office, Kerin. I want to talk to you.' He sounded a little grim.

When they got there he seated her in the chair and leaned on the desk himself, arms folded, looking down at her lifted, enquiring face.

'You didn't faint,' he commented.

'No.'

'Tough, aren't you?' He sounded a little jeering. 'A girl of many talents.'

'Why did you want to see me?' she demanded.

'Can't you guess? Senator Marsh wants to take you to the Pole. It seems you've been a busy little girl these couple of days.'

'Meaning what, exactly?' she challenged him.

'Meaning that Senator Marsh is willing to change his party's planned itinerary and have their plane fly back here after their visit to the Pole station, instead of straight to McMurdo. Because, quote: "That pretty little girl showed us a great time here, and we surely would like to make sure she sees the South Pole before she goes home." Plus a few other complimentary remarks. Congratulations. You've bowled him over, and him with a wife and two kids back home in the States, too.'

'I've done nothing of the kind!' she protested. 'I didn't know he was going to suggest this.'

'What, no dazzling smiles, no regretful hints that you might have to go home without seeing the Pole, none at all?'

'I haven't *hinted*,' she said. 'I did happen to mention that some Antarcticans never get to see the Pole itself. Albie and Belle were both rather—surprised about it. I never expected this!'

'*Albie?*' he queried sarcastically.

'You know very well that doesn't mean a thing!' she said angrily. 'It's been Christian names all round since they arrived. If you want to make something of it, I could just as well accuse *you* of trying to charm Belle Yates. You've certainly been turning some dazzling smiles in *her* direction!'

An arrested look entered his eyes, and for a moment he didn't speak. Then he softly, 'Jealous, Kerin?'

Outraged, she stood up to face him, her eyes almost level with his as he still lounged on the desk. 'That's ridiculous!' she said. 'I'm no more jealous than you are, *Commander!*'

An odd gleam entered his eyes. 'That's an interesting statement. You've yet to call me Dain.'

'What does *that* have to do with it?'

'Not much, perhaps. It might make for a friendlier atmosphere.'

'It might make for a friendlier atmosphere if you would stop throwing innuendoes at me!'

He raised his brows and straightened suddenly, and she stepped back. 'Anyway,' she said, 'I'll tell the Senator I can't go with them.'

'You can.'

Surprised, she stared a moment. 'And have them re-route their plane to fly me back here? Of course I can't!'

'You can't offend our VIP guests. I've already told them you can go. But they'll take you to McMurdo with them, they can transfer you to Scott Base, and you can come back with the next flight that comes to Hillary from there.'

It took two seconds for the implications to hit her. She

took a deep, calming breath and asked, 'And when would that be?'

'I'm not sure. It may be only days.'

'And it may be weeks—or months! Oh, no! You don't get rid of me that easily. I'm staying right here.'

He said, 'You're not. You're doing as you're told.'

'No!'

'I don't like to pull rank, Kerin, but I am in charge here, and *you're going*!'

'All right,' she said, defeated and bitter. 'You've pulled rank. How many strings will you have to pull to make sure I don't come back? I won't make it easy for you, you know.'

Dain gave a sound that was almost a laugh. 'You've never made it easy for me, Kerin.' He paused. 'I won't pull any strings, I give you my word. You can come back just as soon as transport is available.'

She had to believe him, but she was still convinced that it had been his original intention, all the same, to keep her away. Why he had so suddenly capitulated and changed his mind, she couldn't imagine.

Cautiously she asked, 'Is this a new tactic?'

'Tactic?' he repeated. 'Do you suspect my motives?'

'Belle said you were a brilliant strategist.'

'Did she indeed? In what connection?'

'Your asking me to dance last night.'

He smiled a little. 'Belle's more perceptive, perhaps, than you are. Maybe it comes with maturity.'

'I don't think that your intervention was in the least necessary,' she said. 'They were hardly likely to come to blows over me.'

'Maybe not,' he said noncommittally. Then, apparently changing the subject, 'Do you know how the husky got hurt?'

'A dogfight, Mitch said.'

'That's right. The met. party had an eventful trip back. One of the bitches inconveniently became—attractive to the males. A couple of them tried to tear each other apart, competing for her favours. There was complete chaos for a while, I gather, until the men exerted their authority in no uncertain manner, and finally forced the team to settle down. It's the sort of thing we try to avoid, on the ice. Mitch will have to keep the bitch away from the others for a while, until things are back to normal. When she's returned to the lines, she'll be just one of the team again.' His eyes held hers, cold and hard.

She stood looking back at him, a pulse beating hard in her throat, heat stinging at her cheeks. He looked passionless and sure of himself and very slightly disparaging, and she hated him—*hated* him.

'You really are a rotten brute,' she said. 'I'm only sorry that when I come back, you'll still be here!'

She went out of the room without looking at him, but she knew he hadn't moved before she shut the door behind her with a shaking hand.

CHAPTER EIGHT

STANDING on the Polar Plateau, ten thousand feet above
sea level, the snow stretched in an endless vista, rippling and
then smooth in every direction. The most spectacular land-
mark was the glittering silver geodesic dome that housed the
American Amundsen-Scott Base, built to replace the old
station which now lay buried under the snow. The futur-
istic dome, a monument to ingenuity and determination,
was built by American 'seabees' under impossible conditions, their proud welcoming committee told the Senators. Thick gloves had to be worn at all times, and metal
tools had a tendency to grow brittle and snap in the extreme
temperatures.

Kerin tucked her own gloved hands under her well-
padded arms as she trudged behind a cheerful guide towards the tattered red flag on a bamboo stick that in this
white, featureless landscape, marked the spot where Amundsen and Scott had found the South Geographic Pole, in
1912. Now the ice covering had shifted more than three
kilometres, and gradually the great new dome that in 1979
had marked the Pole was also sliding from its position, as
the ice and snow blanket moved over the land more than
seven thousand feet below them.

There was no wind and the temperature was warm for the
Pole, minus eight degrees centigrade. 'The temperatures
here,' their guide said casually, 'average twenty-two degrees colder than in the Arctic.'

'Well, I guess it's a bit of an anti-climax?' Belle asked
Kerin doubtfully as they reached the flag.

'Not a bit,' Kerin smiled. 'At least I can say I've been
here. Besides, it's—awesome,' she added, gesturing at the
vast snow plain about them. 'Isn't it?'

Belle smiled. 'I guess so. But I don't know that I like it.

It makes me feel very ant-like.'

Kerin didn't feel ant-like, she felt alive and exhilarated and curiously buoyant. And very, very glad that she was here, even grateful to Dain Ransome for making her come, as well as to the Americans.

She wondered fleetingly if he would keep his word about not trying to prevent her return. But she wasn't really in doubt. Whatever else, she was certain that Dain Ransome was at least a man of his word. Without in the least understanding his motives, she knew that he had meant it when he had promised not to pull any strings.

The visit to the old Pole concluded, they inspected the buildings housed in the dome, posted letters at the post office to thrill their stay-at-home friends with the unique postmarks, lunched in the mess hall and re-boarded the plane for the flight to McMurdo, the U.S. base only two miles over the hill from Scott.

McMurdo was like a small, snowbound town, albeit an untidy one, with buildings erected apparently without plan, and telegraph wires crisscrossing the streets in seeming confusion. Flocks of skua gulls had abandoned their traditional food-hunting methods on the penguin rookeries in favour of raiding the station's garbage dump, and the brown winged shapes could be seen wheeling and diving against a lowering sky.

The weather worsened as they landed, a vicious wind blowing stinging snow particles against their faces and making them hug their parkas more closely about them. When they reached the welcoming warmth of the buildings at last the shock of the heating and the friendly noise was almost overwhelming. There were more than a dozen women at McMurdo, and Kerin was surprised at the pleasure she found in female company. Maybe Dain had foreseen this. Perhaps he had thought that the delights of such civilisation as the thousand-strong inhabitants of McMurdo enjoyed would make her think twice about returning to the spartan comforts of Hillary. The Americans had a radio station for musical relief, television, and a cinema. Visiting scientists were housed in a hotel, and nobody seemed to think that having women among them was a specially unusual thing. Although the ubiquitous pin-ups that seemed an indispensable part of Polar life appeared here, too, as they had at the Amundsen-Scott station.

When the wind finally died the next day, leaving drifts of snow piled against the base buildings, Kerin travelled back to Williams Field with the Senators' party, and was then taken to Scott base, where she was pleased to find Rose Carson.

'Tell me all about what I'm missing,' Rose begged her cheerfully over a hearty meal in the Scott base mess. 'Should I be sorry I didn't go to Hillary, after all?'

'I don't think so,' Kerin laughed. 'You're probably better off here.'

'Oh? Why's that?'

'Commander Ransome thinks the Antarctic is still a man's world.'

'And you the only woman out there?' exclaimed Rose. 'Oh, dear! Difficult, is he?'

'A bit. Still, when I manage to keep out of his way, it's a great place to be.'

'You won't be able to keep out of anyone's way much in the winter, Kerin. Will you be all right?'

'I'll be all right.'

Rose looked thoughtful. 'Well, this break will do you good. How did you wangle it?'

'I didn't. Senator Marsh suggested it, and Dain Ransome was only too happy to get rid of me for a while. He's hoping I won't come back.' It surprised Kerin how much that hurt, now that she put it into words. She didn't like being unwanted.

'Are you sure you want to go back?' Rose asked.

Kerin hesitated, then said with conviction, 'Yes. Yes, I want to go back. It's where I belong.'

'Belong?'

'I mean, that's where the department sent me,' Kerin said weakly. 'I have a job to do there.'

But she had meant more than that. Deep within there *was* a strong sense of belonging, an affinity with the sense of drive and purpose, the strength, and singlemindedness, and above all the deep, unspoken love of this harsh and unforgiving land that she associated not so much with the station at Hillary as with the man who ran it.

A man who disliked her and distrusted her, a man she had left with a pure, cold flame of hatred in her heart, but who had once shared a secret moment with her, when he had sought her eyes with a silent message—*you, too*.

He didn't come to meet the plane when she arrived back. Les was there, with a slow, broad smile for her, and Eddie with an exuberant hug, picking her up bodily and whirling her round before he set her back on her booted feet. Nat Mitchell's white grin split the black curls of his beard when he greeted her, and Guy Halsey boldly kissed her mouth, saying, 'Hey, we missed you, Kerin.'

Smilingly, she stepped back from the unexpected embrace. 'Obviously! I'm flattered, Guy.'

Apparently not to be outdone, Sebastian grabbed her waist and planted a loud kiss on her cheek, his blond beard harsh against her skin.

'You're a sight for sore eyes,' he told her enthusiastically, awaking an echo in her memory, of a time when Dain had said that to her, adding, '*And you don't know how sincerely I mean that.*' He had just come back, of course, from his last Antarctic stint. Even the man of ice had enjoyed the sight of a pretty girl after his long deprivation of feminine company.

He must have known she was back, but apparently he could do without the sight of her now. She didn't see him until that evening, in the mess.

He stopped in the doorway when he saw her, and she looked up from the plate she had in front of her straight into his eyes, as coolly expressionless as she had ever seen them.

Nothing's changed, she thought, and turned to answer

some remark of Eddie's with an absent-minded affirmative, as out of the corner of her eye she saw Dain cross the room to the serving hatch.

But he came and pulled out a chair opposite her, then, saying levelly, 'Hello, Kerin. How was the Pole?'

'Cold,' she said, glancing his way briefly and carefully pushing peas on to her fork.

'Is that all?'

She looked up at him then, and said simply, 'No. It was fantastic.'

A faint gleam of satisfaction warmed his eyes, and he gave her the barest nod. 'I thought you wouldn't want to miss it,' he said.

'Nothin' much to see but the seabees' dome, though, is there!' Eddie put in.

Dain was still looking at Kerin, and once again that extraordinary current of understanding flowed, for an instant, between them. Nothing much to see, as Eddie said, but everything to feel, to imagine. The terrible power of the pitiless land, and the stubborn pride of the men who had set out to conquer it, the triumph and tragedy of those who had made incredible journeys to reach that mystic centre of the earth, where, as Eddie complained, there was 'nothing to see.' Kerin had felt it all, standing there on the ice-cap. And Dain Ransome knew it.

Eddie asked, 'How was McMurdo?' And she wrenched her gaze from Dain's and said, 'Warmer. And fantastic, too, in its way. But I'm glad to be back.'

Eddie chuckled and said, 'You hear that, Dain? She likes us!'

'Do you, Kerin?' asked Dain, mockery in his voice.

She was spared having to answer that, because Eddie was saying happily, 'We should have a party to welcome Kerin home.' And before either of them could demur, he stood up and shouted, 'Hey, boys! How about a party? Kerin's home!'

There was a goodnatured chorus of assent, and one or two lighthearted whoops and whistles, and Kerin smiled back her appreciation at them, not daring to look at Dain.

They made it an evening to remember. Someone played the piano in one corner of the mess, and another man brought out a piano accordion. There were two guitars and a violin, and everyone joined a rowdy singalong.

Someone found a beer bottle and started a competition to see how many matches could be stacked on the open top before they fell, and then someone else challenged them all with a matchstick puzzle that Dain watched half a dozen of them fail at before he stepped in and solved it with a few well-thought-out moves.

One of the guitarists sang some popular folksongs and was enthusiastically applauded, and the pianist rendered *Claire de Lune* while they hushed appreciatively, before swinging into another medley of singalong songs. Another man found a broom and started a limbo competition that was a cause of great hilarity. Kerin laughed and clapped the last few who managed to inch under the broom, and applauded the eventual winner, but refused to join in. Dain had stayed quite close to her all evening, but she didn't need to look at him to know he would disapprove of *that*!

It was midnight when the party broke up, at Dain's easy suggestion that Kerin's day had been a long one, and she found herself walking with him through the eerie twilight outside, the snow gently crackling under their booted feet.

He came with her into the cold-porch outside her hut, and in the gloom she turned to him and said, rather formally, 'Thanks for seeing me home, Commander.'

'My pleasure,' he said with slight mockery, leaning his tall shape against the door frame. 'How was the social life at Ross Island?'

'Not very social,' she shrugged. 'Everybody's busy. We talked quite a lot.'

'Talked?' he queried. 'No dancing? No light flirtations in the midnight sun?'

She was still and silent for a moment. Then she said

with soft pleading, 'Oh, please, Dain! It was a lovely party. Please don't spoil it.'

There was a heartbeat's silence when he didn't move. Then he straightened away from the door and she felt his hands on her shoulders, propelling her towards him. He said, 'Goodnight, Kerin,' and then his lips met hers, warm and compelling, briefly passionate. Then his head lifted and she heard him say, 'Welcome home,' before he released her and was suddenly gone.

She had been away two weeks, and in spite of the greater variety of people and entertainment at McMurdo and Scott, the time had seemed to drag. They had taken her to see the historic huts that Scott and Shackleton had used on their epic journeys, the food on the shelves still preserved in the natural deep-freeze atmosphere, magazines dated 1907 on Shackleton's table, and boots and socks casually lying about as though their owners had just stepped out for a few moments.

And she had seen for herself the fabulous ice caves that Dain Ransome had described in his talk, sliding down through the hole in the snow to enter an eerie blue-green world of caverns and passages hung with ice stalactites, into a magnificent central cave in which the ice columns from floor to ceiling, the glittering forms and shapes glowing in the lamplight, made an incredible glass palace; the only sound the snapping of cracking ice.

She was glad to have seen it, but all the time she could hear in her mind an echo of Dain Ransome's voice, describing all this with a controlled passion of awe, and there was restlessness within her, almost a longing, as though the experience would have been more satisfying, more complete, if only he had been by her side.

Now she wondered if that brief kiss had meant that he was glad to see her back, after all. She hadn't thought so, when she had first seen him in the mess, and although he had scarcely left her side, she had felt it was less from a desire for her company than from his ingrained distrust of her. In an apparently easy-going way he had successfully kept the others at a distance from her, pleasantly vetoing Guy's suggestion of dancing, adroitly changing the subject when Eddie made some broad remark about missing having a woman about, making sure she strolled about and talked to everyone, changing her seat often so that no one had a chance to monopolise her. Except, in a way, himself. Although he had scarcely spoken to her. He had just been— *there*.

She quickly slipped into the routine of the station, watching as unobtrusively as possible, and asking questions of the men about their work. The scientists, of course, were all specialists in their own fields, and all enthusiastic at the chance to work in the giant natural laboratory of the Antarctic continent. She was able to go out with some of the field parties and watch them at work, gathering important data on weather conditions, rock formations, the nature of ice crystals, even on the meagre plant life that managed to survive the incredible cold, and the minute insects that spent the winter literally frozen in their tracks, to revive in the warmth of the spring sunshine.

Guy and Sebastian had left to camp for a week at a penguin rookery which they were studying, when a visiting scientist arrived from a Norwegian base. He was interested in penguins, and Dain arranged a helicopter for him to be flown out to the rookery, accompanied by himself and Kerin.

They had to land at a distance from the penguin colony. Kerin had heard horrific stories of thoughtless pilots putting down too close, stampeding thousands of terrified birds across the ice shelf and into the sea perhaps several miles off, leaving their eggs and chicks to the mercy of the cold and the skua gulls that preyed on them.

The party trudged across the snow to arrive at last on a tongue of bare, snow-drifted grey rock where the scientists were huddled against the wind in a lean-to of canvas, laboriously making notes with gloved fingers on the movements and habits of the odd little creatures who built their nests here every year.

The stench was at first overwhelming, and Kerin saw Sebastian give her a sly grin, which she returned with a rueful one of her own. But she soon forgot that in the fascination of listening to him and the other man talk about the penguins.

'The nests are pretty well completed,' Sebastian said, 'and some have eggs already.'

'They don't look very comfortable,' Kerin commented, looking at the untidy ring of stones that constituted a nest.

'These are Antarctic creatures,' Dain reminded them. 'Like everything else that belongs here, they're extremely hardy.'

'But these little Adelies are not quite as tough as the big Emperor penguins,' Sebastian added. 'The Emperors actually hatch their chicks in the winter, on the ice. The male incubates the egg over two months, living on his body fat, while the female returns to the sea, and after two months brings back food for the newly hatched young.'

'I'm sure you approve of that division of labour, Kerin,' said Dain, and she looked up to see a faint smile on his lips, a teasing light in his eyes.

Tentatively she smiled back at him. He didn't often smile at her and his eyes were usually coldly expressionless when he looked at her. 'If both the partners are happy about it,' she said. 'Why not?'

She thought he looked speculative, but he turned away then as one of the other men spoke to him, and she returned her attention to the penguins. There were hundreds of them, and the grey rock was a mass of activity, waving heads and waddling bodies, flippers absurdly flapping here and there as some indignant nestholder repelled a neighbour who strayed too close, or two inhabitants engaged in what appeared to be a cosy gossip.

The talk behind her had become technical, and later she would have to take some notes and get them to reduce their scientific jargon to more readily understandable terms. Just now she was content to watch the penguins, and the occasional wheeling, graceful skua casting an ominous shadow over the rock, looking for an egg that might have rolled away from a poorly constructed nest ...

Then she realised that Guy had settled himself beside her, and she turned her head to smile at him absently.

'Cute little beggars, aren't they?' he said.

'Yes. They're a sort of symbol of Antarctica. Are you enjoying working here?'

Guy grimaced. 'It's not too bad when the weather's fine. I'll be glad to get back to base—and you—though.'

He lifted a gloved hand and touched her cheek. Guy was a bit of a flirt, she thought, slightly amused, as she shook her head and smiled at him again.

But the amusement died suddenly as she turned her head and caught a glacial look from Dain. Did he think she was encouraging the young assistant?

Let him think, then, she told herself crossly. Whatever she did he treated her with the same aloof contempt, most of the time, except on the rare occasions when he seemed to thaw into some semblance of normal humanity.

But all the same, she made sure that when Sebastian had finished explaining things to the Norwegian she had questions to ask that kept him talking for a time to her. Dain would have no cause to accuse her of favouritism.

It didn't seem to help, though, and on the way back to the base Dain scarcely spoke to her. Which was fine with her, she told herself fiercely. Just fine.

Mitch taught her how to drive a dog team, and she was delighted to find that she handled them well, earning his high praise. There was something tremendously exhilarating about riding behind the dogs as they trotted, panting and happy, across an expanse of snow, the mountains in the distance seeming much closer than they really were in the clear, dust-free air, the uneven bumping of the runners mingling with the sound of the dogs' breathing, and the thin cries from the handler. It wasn't really a fast ride, but it had a thrill all its own.

On blizzard days, the dogs curled themselves into the snow and wrapped their bushy tails about their noses to protect them, then let the snow blow over them until they shook themselves free of it when the storm was over.

These were the days when the men worked inside, and the field parties camping out sometimes couldn't get their radio messages through, while they huddled in their tents waiting for the weather to clear.

But when it was fine and clear, the ice shelf took on a myriad jewel colours, subtle blues and greens and gold lights from the sun, even deep mossy greens about the sea where the towering cliffs of ice plunged into the calm, mysterious waters, and sometimes pink and orange tints from the minerals that the meltwater carried to the sea.

Sometimes a polar mirage appeared strangely on the horizon, mountains floating in the air, or the base buildings from a distance suddenly acquiring a mirror-image that hovered upside down above them, and occasionally the sun danced through a cluster of ice-crystals that hung in the air, winking off their gem-like facets and showing up their breathtaking, delicate beauty.

Kerin had been out driving the team with Mitch one evening, and she went to the mess afterwards for a thirst-quenching drink of fruit juice. As she entered the warm atmosphere she thought at first that the room was deserted, although a record was playing a haunting orchestral piece on the stereo.

Then she saw that Dain was there, lounging back on the sofa in one corner, his eyes closed, head tipped back on clasped hands.

She had never seen him like that, relaxed, oblivious, off guard, and she stopped and stared, fascinated despite herself. His hair was quite long now, touching his collar, and it waved a little over his brow, a strand or two brushing his forehead and touched his straight brown eyebrows. His mouth looked less stern in sleep, its moulded contours almost betraying a softening, as though when he woke it might curve into a smile.

He stirred, and in sudden panic she stepped back, knocking a chair and making a noise that brought his eyes open instantly, pinning her with a blue shaft of accusation.

His brows went up, and she said, 'I'm sorry. I didn't mean to wake you.'

'How long have you been there?'

'I just came in,' she said. 'To get some fruit juice.'

'Would you get me some?' he asked, not moving.

'All right.'

She poured two glasses and when she came back to the sofa and handed him one, he said, 'Sit down,' and indicated the place beside him.

Kerin hesitated and then obeyed, sipping at her glass. The liquid was cool and refreshing.

The music swelled in a lyrical crescendo, and she asked softly, 'What is that piece?'

'*Sinfonia Antarctica*, by Vaughan Williams,' he told her.

'I might have known,' she murmured against the background of the music.

'Known what?'

'Do you ever think of anything but Antarctica?'

He took some of his drink and turned deliberately to look at her. 'Frequently. Don't you like the music?'

She listened for a few moments more before she said, 'I love it.'

'Yes,' he said quietly, 'I thought you would.'

She looked up at him questioningly, but he didn't expand. A faint warmth stirred in her, a gladness. Dain had expected her to like the music because he knew how she felt about the Antarctic, how it stirred her with its strangeness and its beauty and its implacable purity. He knew.

As though he could read her thoughts, he said, 'You haven't seen the winter yet. This is the soft side of Antarctica, the summer.'

'Is that a gypsy's warning?' she asked lightly.

'Would you listen to a warning?'

'Not if it's meant to frighten me away before the winter,' she said.

'You don't frighten easily, do you, Kerin?' His tone was mocking, but his mouth almost smiled.

'No,' she said, 'I don't.' She was looking straight at him, her head tilted up, proudly challenging.

Softly he murmured, 'I wonder what it would take——' And his free hand reached up and curved about her neck, his fingers hard at her nape, his thumb gently pressing the base of her throat.

Her heart made a liar of her, bumping in sudden fear, but her voice was steady as she said on a deliberately mocking note, 'You wouldn't go as far as murder to get rid of me, would you?'

'No. But there are other measures available. Doesn't it occur to you that I'm a lot stronger than you are?'

'If you're talking about brute force,' she said, 'I daresay you are. It doesn't scare me.'

His eyes had narrowed a little. 'It doesn't scare you because you're sure I'd never exercise it,' he told her. 'What makes you so certain that I'm bound by the usual rules of so-called civilised behaviour?' His thumb was moving on her throat, but there was something vaguely threatening in the caressing movement. 'I've spent a lot of time in the Antarctic,' he mused. 'It isn't strictly true what you said that first day about the Dependency being under New Zealand law. The status of the law is a bit vague here. The perspective on crime is altered, where stealing a man's parka is tantamount to murder.'

Uneasy, Kerin made a restless, experimental movement, trying to draw away.

As though he had been waiting for it, his fingers instantly tightened. His thumb exerted a slight pressure at the base of her throat, and he said, a faint hint of cruelty etching the smile on his mouth, 'What could you do to stop me if——'

'*This!*' she said fiercely, and threw the remainder of her drink into his face.

She saw the total blankness of shock before he moved his hand from her to wipe his sleeve across his face, and as she gathered her muscles, preparing for flight, was startled by the sound of his ringing laughter.

Totally surprised, Kerin stayed where she was while Dain put his drink down on the nearest table and got up to fetch a paper table napkin and mop up the wetness from his face and throat.

Then he turned to her, laughter still in his eyes, and it did something strange to her heart, because she had never seen him look like that. He crumpled the paper into a ball and threw it carelessly down on the table and came towards her with an air of purpose.

'You did ask for it,' she whispered, feeling strangely breathless, her voice almost pleading.

'Oh, yes,' he admitted casually. 'But you should have run when you had the chance.' He bent and took the empty glass from her hand.

She made to rise then, but he moved swiftly, with beautiful economy, and somehow she found herself tipped sideways and backward until she was lying on the sofa, with the considerable length of Dain's powerful body pinning her to it, inescapably.

She squirmed in panic, tried to say, *'Don't!'* and found her protest stopped decisively as his mouth found hers with devastating precision. She tried to resist him, her body stiff against him, clenched fists held in his long fingers, tiny sounds of protest strangled in her throat.

He took not the least bit of notice, his mouth exploiting the softness of hers with frank sensual enjoyment. She tried to jerk her head aside, and his mouth pressed harder, pushing her head back into the cushion behind it, and his teeth briefly nipped her lower lip, a small, painful punishment that brought a choked gasp to her throat but didn't break the skin. And immediately afterwards his lips replaced the sharpness of his teeth, firmly, then gentle, then dizzyingly possessive, until they moved and opened on hers, parting her mouth imperatively until she moaned deeply and stopped trying to fight him.

Only when at last she lay quiescent and limp in his arms did he lift his head, releasing her mouth, and looking down at her with eyes darkened by passion.

Kerin looked back at him, touching her tongue to her throbbing mouth, feeling his nearness with every inch of her body, her mind appalled at the feelings that nearness was evoking.

Trying to regain some measure of sanity, she said, her voice hard with effort, 'All right, Commander, you've had your revenge. Satisfied?'

He gave a small laugh, and moved, letting her sit up. She didn't dare try to stand, yet, afraid her legs might not support her. She felt shattered.

Dain was leaning back against the corner of the sofa, his arm along the back, looking at her with narrowed eyes, a faint glitter in the blue depths of them. 'Was it so bad?' he asked softly. 'I might have been tempted to hit you instead.'

'And I might have preferred that!' she said tartly.

'I don't believe you,' he said quietly.

'You don't know how it feels,' she said, 'for a woman to be kissed against her will. A slap would have been less— humiliating.'

'Humiliating?'

Her glance challenged him. 'Don't pretend you didn't intend just that. You meant it as a punishment.'

'A sweet revenge, yes. Did you expect to be allowed to get away with what you did? I don't make allowances for women—you know that.'

'You just treat them differently.'

He shrugged. 'Call it conditioning if you like, I don't see myself giving a woman a crack on the jaw. No matter how much she deserves it.'

'And you thought *I* did?'

He stood up suddenly. 'I think you'd better go to bed.'

Kerin watched him stride over to the stereo turntable, and realised the music had stopped. Uncertainly she stood up, picked up the two glasses and carried them to the kitchen hatch. He was ignoring her, carefully sliding the record into its sleeve.

She went to the door, walking carefully, and said 'Good-night.'

Dain didn't reply.

CHAPTER NINE

AFTER that evening Kerin avoided being alone with Dain, immersing herself in the busy life of the base. Once when she came back with Mitch with a dead seal tied to the sled, she noticed Dain looking at her thoughtfully, perhaps with some curiosity, but he turned away when her eyes met his. She hoped Mitch wouldn't mention that she had turned away as he fired the shot that killed the seal. The dogs had to be fed, and international regulations decreed exactly how many seals might be killed to ensure fresh meat to augment their diet of pemmican, but she couldn't help feeling a little sickened by the necessary killing.

Not that killing was confined to men, in the Antarctic. She had watched a leopard seal bite the head from a penguin and shake it out of its skin with deadly economy and skill, seen a young seal taken by a killer whale, and swallowed down a rising sickness as a sharp-beaked skua gull cruelly dug a half-formed chick from an abandoned penguin egg. The wages of carelessness in this harsh, unforgiving land was death.

Christmas was the next milestone in their lives, celebrated with an enormous Christmas dinner and a day off for everyone. In the evening Dain read the Christmas story from the Bible in his beautiful voice to a silent assembly, and then they sang Christmas carols, and later, other songs, until it naturally became a party.

There had been mail, special treats and parcels from home, and everyone was in high spirits. A couple of the men drank a little too much, and Guy became a little too amorous, so that Kerin had to tactfully fend him off. He certainly had a weakness for women, she thought resignedly, as well as being inclined to over-indulge in alcohol whenever the occasion offered an excuse. It was just possible that

116

Belle and Dain had been right about that other time—he might have created an awkward situation.

He was glowering, rather, now, in the corner where she had left him, staring into his drink, but now and then raising his head to give her a smouldering look as she sat chatting to Eddie and one of the marine biologists.

'That's where the food chain begins,' the biologist was saying. 'Floating diatoms, simple plants, feed krill, which is eaten by the fish and squid, which in turn are eaten by the penguins, whales, and seals—though some of them eat krill as well. And then you have the seabirds which manure what plants there are, and the insects feed on *them*.'

'I see,' murmured Kerin, as she saw Guy, across the room, rise unsteadily to his feet, moving towards them.

'What we're trying to do,' the biologist went on earnestly, and Kerin looked back at him as Dain swiftly rose and blocked Guy from her view, taking his arm. 'What we're trying to do is chart exactly the intermingling, the *interdependency* of life-forms in an unexploited environment. What we learn here about food chains could save the world from starvation. We could learn how to farm the oceans.'

'That's marvellous,' Kerin told him, as from the corner of her eye she followed Guy's and Dain's movement towards another group of men.

'Of course, what's great about *this* place,' the man went on, 'is that it's relatively unpolluted. At McMurdo Sound you can hardly see the sea-bed any more for all the rubbish that's been dropped there.'

Her attention caught, Kerin said, 'What?'

'Pollution,' the man explained. 'It's a problem. Like, nothing decays here, you see. For years the way to get rid of any sort of rubbish, including beer cans and everything else, was to leave it on the ice and let it drop to the sea-bed when the ice melted, either as is or in barrels. The whole ecology of that area has been affected. One thing about Ransome, he insisted on a decent incinerator, a small crushing plant, and at least some of the rubbish being removed from the area by plane. I tell you, diving here is a pleasure—under the ice, the sea-bed is purely beautiful!'

'I'd like to see it,' said Kerin, half an idea forming in her mind.

The man grinned. 'Under the ice-shelf?'

His scepticism was showing, putting her on her mettle. 'Why not?' she asked. 'I've done a fair bit of diving.'

'You have? Well——' the man looked doubtful. Then, his eagerness for the job overcoming his scruples, he said, 'Look, if you could help a bit—it's just a matter of collecting, you know, scooping up netfulls of stuff. We sort it later. But another diver now and then—well, frankly, it would be marvellous. The limit in these waters is thirty minutes.'

Eddie said, 'Do you keep to it?'

'Pretty well,' the biologist grinned. 'But we've all overstayed at some time, I guess. Down there it's another world, and hard to keep track of time.'

A few days later, encased in insulated rubber from head to toe, Kerin stood on the edge of a hole cut in the ice and adjusted the heavy oxygen tank on her back, trying not to look as nervously excited as she felt. Her partner made a thumbs-up sign, and fell into the hole, and a few seconds later she braced herself and followed him.

It was indeed another world, silent and dimly glowing. The water was amazingly clear and the sea-bed seemed to stretch for miles. There were shoals of fish and the tiny krill floated by in clouds, the ice sheet above them was translucent white, and the water limpidly green. There were tiny blue starfish and larger orange ones with spidery tentacles moving gently on the uneven surface of the sea-bed, spiny urchins, and jellyfish.

Back on the snow after thirty minutes, the white glare dazzled and hurt her eyes, and she was glad to don sunglasses for the journey back to base.

That evening Dain stopped her as she was leaving the mess after dinner. 'I hear you've been diving?' he said, his voice hostile.

'That's right.' She was wary, wondering why he seemed to dislike the idea.

'I don't want you to do that again,' he said.

'*What?*'

'You heard me,' he said tersely. 'You're not a scientist, you're Information Officer, that's all. I know scuba diving is a hobby of yours, but these men have *work* to do down there. This isn't one of your tropical holiday resorts.'

Enraged, Kerin clenched her fists and tried to speak calmly. 'You've misunderstood, Mr Ransome. I was asked to help, because an extra diver is useful in these conditions. I wasn't just along for the ride.'

'You already have a job to do.' He kept his voice low, but she knew that he, too, was angry. 'I'd rather you stuck to your own work and left the men to theirs.'

'Why? You said yourself, there's no union demarcation here. Everyone helps out wherever they can.'

He looked at her in silence for a moment, then said stiffly, 'All right. But remember that diving in sub-zero temperatures is especially risky, and stick to the rules.'

'I will,' she promised.

And she did, until the day she was swimming under the ice, her partner in the distance filling a net with specimens from the sea-bed, and a dark sinuous shape swam suddenly close, seemingly from nowhere—a seal, its movements in the water utterly graceful, a dreamlike ballet in slow motion. Her partner signalled her, and she indicated by signs that she was coming, but her movement was slow, as the seal still captivated her attention, swimming closer now, turning swift somersaults in the water, its sleek body twisting and curving, diving and arrowing upwards to the ice, executing a fast, corkscrewing movement and then folding its flippers to dive again.

It was a dazzling performance, and though she moved slowly until she neared the hole where they had entered the water, Kerin lingered a while to watch it.

Then a dark shape dropped beside her, and she realised

her partner had returned and was urgently signalling her to get out.

Reluctantly she moved her flippered feet to take her to the surface and put up a hand to be helped out of the icy water.

She was surprised at the almost rough strength of the hand that took hers and hauled her out on to the ice. As the water streamed and froze on her goggles she caught a glimpse of pale hair and a pair of blazing eyes. She raised a hand and pushed the goggles away, and Dain said, 'When you've changed, I want to see you. In my office.'

When she had dressed in warm trousers and a thick wool sweater, combed out her hair and used some make-up to hide pale cheeks and colour her lips, she found Dain waiting for her with a forbidding coldness in his expression.

Calmly she said, 'You wanted to speak to me?'

'Yes. I told you when you started this diving stunt that you'd better stick to the rules. You were down there for forty minutes. This is the last time, Kerin, and that's final. Understood?'

'Oh, for heaven's sake!' she exclaimed. 'Everyone breaks the rules now and then——'

'Not when I'm in charge, they don't! Not more than once. And you've had your chance.'

He looked pretty implacable, and she swallowed her anger and tried sweet reason. 'It *was* only ten minutes,' she reminded him. 'I'm sorry, I was watching a seal and I didn't realise how long I'd been under the water. Surely you can understand that?'

She thought his face softened a little, but not much. 'I understand, all right,' he said. 'But that doesn't alter the facts. You don't get another chance to put me through——'

Puzzled as he stopped abruptly there, she asked, 'When did you arrive?'

'Soon after you went in. They told me you'd been down five minutes. We waited, and your partner came up. And then we waited for you. You were a hell of a long time deciding to follow him. How long would you have stayed down if he hadn't come to fetch you?'

'I was just coming,' she said defensively. 'Were you worried?'

'*Of course* I was worried, you little idiot!' More quietly, he went on, 'I'm responsible, ultimately, for the safety of everyone on this base. What do you *think* I felt while you were watching your damned seal?'

'I'm sorry,' Kerin told him again. 'I promise I won't do it again.'

'I don't need your promise,' he told her. 'You're not diving again, and that's an order.'

Her lips tightened at the autocratic note, but he was within his rights, she supposed. 'All right,' she said. 'You make yourself very clear. But I want it understood that I think you're being rigid and unreasonable.'

Dain looked at her and gave a small nod. 'Understood,' he said curtly. 'Have you had a hot drink since you came in?'

'No. I'm all right—I'm quite warm now.'

'Go and get——' He stopped and gave her a surprising, wry smile. 'I think,' he said, 'you should have one. Will you take the advice of an old Antarctic hand, and get yourself something?'

She supposed it was a sort of olive branch, but she was still too disappointed and angry to accept it graciously. She said stiffly that she would, and then left without looking at him again.

Les Howard had returned that day with a party from Marie Byrd Land where they had been doing a survey for mapping. When Kerin went to the mess to make some coffee he was there, having a can of beer.

'Something upset you?' he asked, after she had greeted him almost absently.

'Does it show?' she smiled at him ruefully. 'I've just been told off and had my privileges withdrawn.'

'Dain?'

'Yes.' She told him the whole story and he looked sympathetic, but said, 'I told you, Ransome's tough, but a good leader.'

Kerin sighed. 'Doesn't he ever make a concession—a compromise?'

Les grinned. 'It has been known. If he didn't know when to bend the rules a little, he wouldn't be such a good man in command.'

Kerin chewed her lip. 'You know him pretty well,' she said softly. 'Don't you? I suppose you wouldn't——'

'No, I wouldn't,' Les said bluntly, holding up a hand. 'One thing that cuts no ice with Dain is anyone asking for special favours—for themselves or anyone else. And don't get any ideas about batting those long eyelashes at him, either. *That's* guaranteed to fail!'

Indignantly she looked up at him. 'I didn't have any such idea! For one thing, I'm not the type, and for another, the man's made of ice!'

'Sorry!' Les apologised, laughing a little. 'I guess you're not the devious sort of female, trading on your sex. The trouble is, Dain thinks there isn't any other kind, barring a few who married the likes of me. But I wouldn't count on that last statement of yours, Kerin. Ever seen a volcano inside a snow-covered mountain?'

Looking at him doubtfully, she said, 'Why doesn't he trust women, Les?'

Her companion looked uncomfortable and muttered that he hadn't exactly said that, had he? And although she tried to press him, he laughed and shook his head and clumsily but effectively changed the subject.

They were not short of visitors, for all the important tourists sent by various governments were curious about the newest Antarctic station and tried to include it in their itineraries. The Antarcticans called them 'tourists' although ostensibly everyone had a good reason for visiting the region, and many expected VIP treatment when they got there.

In January Kerin paid another visit to the penguin rookery when Eddie flew out some mail and supplies to a party which had been there for a number of weeks.

Dain came aboard almost at the last minute, and as they lifted off she wondered why Eddie hadn't mentioned that he was coming. If she had known she might have skipped the trip herself.

The chicks had hatched now and the females had returned to share the burden of parenthood with the fathers. Small fluffy balls of grey down crawled in and out from the stone nests, and occasionally an unwary chick or a careless parent invited the attention of the ominous skuas that perched on nearby rocks, ready to soar and dive and take off again with a helpless baby penguin clutched in a strong beak. *Their* young had to eat, too.

Kerin watched as an adult penguin squabbled with a neighbour, leaving its nest unattended, and leaned forward anxiously as the baby looked about curiously and then lurched unsteadily off the nest and began wandering across the rock. The biologists were busy making notes, and Eddie, saying he had seen everything there was to see already, had stayed in the biologists' small hut, reading some girlie magazines.

But when she gasped and made to move forward, Dain caught at her arm. 'Where are you going?' he asked.

'That baby—he'll get lost.'

His grip tightened. 'Leave it.'

'But——' She strained against his hold.

'We're scientists,' he said. 'We're not here to interfere. We record the way things are, not change them.'

'I just want to put one chick back on its nest!' she protested.

'And in the process maybe frighten a whole lot of other parent birds off theirs! Sit still, and remember you can't change the course of nature.'

Resentfully, Kerin subsided, then gasped in horror as a slim, swift shadow passed over the chick and the winged nemesis dropped from the sky on its terrified head.

There was nothing quick or merciful about the chick's death, and when the pathetic corpse at last lay still and bleeding against the rock, Kerin felt sick and cold. Her mittened hands were clenched until they ached, and her face felt clammy. Unfairly, she hated the skua for a savagery it could not help, and equally unfairly, she hated Dain Ransome, not so much because he had stopped her from rescuing the chick, but in an obscure way because she knew if he had not been there she would have closed her eyes and at least been spared the full horror of those few minutes when the poor creature had struggled helplessly against its fate.

When it was all over, she wouldn't meet his eyes, although she knew he was looking at her. She thought he wanted to see how it had affected her, that he was waiting for her to show the weakness of woman that he expected from her, and she wasn't going to give him that satisfaction.

A few minutes later he touched her arm and said, 'Let's go.'

She stood up, still not looking at him, but when he said, 'All right?' she carefully made her face blank and faintly surprised and answered, 'Of course.'

They said goodbye to the biologists, who scarcely seemed to notice their going anyway, and returned to the camp, and Eddie.

One of the huskies had a litter of four blind, fluffy pups. Mitch was as proud as a new father, and the mess toasted him and the pups in celebration.

They were kept in the warmth of the sled room, with their mother, and Kerin took a particular fancy to the longest-haired one, which was a little smaller than the others and a particularly attractive pale golden colour with dark tips on its furry coat.

Mitch looked at the pup doubtfully and muttered, 'Coat's too long.'

'Too long?' Kerin queried, surprised. 'I thought they had to be shaggy to keep out the cold.'

'Not too shaggy. They can get iced up too easily. Then they've been known to tear their flesh badly trying to get themselves out of the ice.'

'I see. But he's certainly a beauty, isn't he?'

'Mm. Well, we'll see how he goes,' Mitch said vaguely.

Once the pups opened their eyes they were allowed the run of the building, and became favourites with the men, tumbling into mischief at every opportunity but being tolerated for the sake of their youth and undoubted charm.

At six weeks, when the summer was drawing to its close, the pups were being weaned. Kerin was allowed to help feed them bowls of chopped seal meat and milk.

'They're darlings!' she said to Mitch, as they watched the pups scrambling over each other to get their meal. Already there were signs that one was going to be king of the litter. His miniature snarls and snaps seemed to intimidate his brothers and one sister quite effectively. 'He's a bully!' she laughed.

'Just showing 'em who's boss,' Mitch grinned. 'One day that one will grow up to challenge his own father.' He looked up as a footstep thudded on the board floor. 'Hello, Dain!'

Kerin didn't look up until Dain came to stand beside her, and then he wasn't looking at her, but staring down at the pups. He turned to Mitch and commented, 'I thought you were going to get rid of one?'

Mitch looked oddly embarrassed, and shot a glance at Kerin—why, she couldn't fathom. 'Thought I'd wait a bit,' he muttered.

'Why?' Dain asked uncompromisingly. 'I understood you thought the pup was too long-haired. It won't grow any shorter, will it?'

Mitch shifted uncomfortably on his feet. 'Well, they're all inclined to be a bit more fluffy when they're young. I thought he might outgrow it a bit, in time.'

'Any sign of it?'

Mitch hesitated. 'No.'

'How long are you going to wait?'

'Oh, well—maybe a couple of weeks. Actually, I know I should have done it before, but he's a cute little beggar, and then—Well, Kerin's fond of him, you know.'

Dain swung round then, pinning Kerin's startled eyes with his. 'I might have known!' he said softly. Turning back to the dog-handler, he said, 'If you're sure *now* the animal will never be any good for a team, then get *rid* of him *now*. You know we can't afford to feed a dog that's not going to be any use.'

He swung away and left the room, and Mitch looked sheepishly at Kerin. 'He's right, of course. I should have got rid of the little fellow before his eyes opened. I knew then that he'd have to go eventually.'

Around a lump in her throat, Kerin said, 'I didn't realise. You kept him for my sake?'

The man shrugged. 'Sort of. Stupid of me to keep putting it off. I've known all along——'

'Oh, Mitch!' she exclaimed. 'You're an idiot! But a very nice one.'

She gave him a quick peck on his bewhiskered cheek and followed Dain.

He must have walked away very fast. At first she couldn't see him at all, then she saw a glint of fair hair over by one of the other buildings, where he stood talking to one of the men.

Kerin walked over that way slowly, not wanting to interrupt, but with a vague idea of explaining to Dain that it hadn't been her idea to keep the pup. The thought of it being put down made her feel sickly miserable, but it wasn't fair if he was blaming her, as his words had seemed to indicate.

She hadn't reached them when Dain nodded to the other man and turned away, glancing briefly in her direction before he deliberately turned away to go into the nearby building.

Kerin stopped walking, and the other man cast a curious glance at her, hesitated, then moved off in the other direction.

She remained standing on the sunlit snow, trying to tell herself that Dain couldn't have deliberately snubbed her, that of course he hadn't realised she had wanted to speak to him. And knowing that of course, he *had*. That he had deliberately walked away to avoid her.

Well, she wasn't chasing after the man, she thought indignantly, for anything. He wouldn't be able to avoid her for ever.

She stopped him that evening as he was leaving the mess, noting the fleeting irritation that crossed his lean face when she asked, 'May I talk to you for a moment, Commander?'

But he said, 'Sure. What is it?'

Kerin hesitated at the near-hostility of his tone, and he added, 'If you're going to ask for a reprieve for that pup, the answer is a definite no. It would have been easier all round if Mitch had been sensible in the first place—it constantly amazes me the way the toughest, most down-to-earth types will melt at the sight of a feminine tear.'

'You've got it wrong,' she said. 'I didn't ask Mitch to save the pup. And I'm not asking for a reprieve, either.'

He looked sceptical. 'Mitch said the pup was a favourite of yours.'

'He is. But I didn't know he should have been destroyed.'

'Mitch wouldn't have kept him if it hadn't been for you.'

'All right,' she retorted, with a glimmer of temper, 'that's probably so. But I think it's unreasonable to hold me responsible for other people's actions.'

'Why?'

'Why? Surely that's obvious. Les said you'd be a fair leader.'

His eyes narrowed slightly. 'And you think I'm not?'

'Not to me. You make me a scapegoat.'

'You're wrong,' he said, a glint of cold anger in his eyes. 'I've done my damnedest to be fair with you, but I also see that some of the things the men do are a direct result of your presence. And I have very good reason to believe that you're not above using your feminine charm deliberately to get what you want.'

'*What* reason?' she asked, astounded.

'Your own words.' He looked down into her widened eyes and said, 'I heard you talking to Val Lamont that day we met. I couldn't catch all that you were saying, but the gist was very clear. As I remember, you were describing how you intended to use all your feminine allure to get what you wanted from me.'

Suddenly enlightened, she exclaimed, '*That* was why you snubbed me so thoroughly after the lecture?'

'I don't like being manipulated, or flattered. You did lay it on a bit thick about how you enjoyed the lecture.'

But she hadn't been 'laying it on' at all. Her enthusiasm had been quite sincere. 'But you're wrong,' she said. 'Have you been holding that silly conversation against me all this time? Is that why you didn't want me here?'

She didn't like the line of his mouth as he raised his eyebrows at her. Then he said, 'You flatter yourself. It wasn't that important. I've told you why I object to your presence here.'

'Oh, yes,' she said. 'I'm female and therefore a disruptive influence.'

'A certain type of female,' he corrected.

'That sort of generalisation is typical of the way your mind works,' she told him, her voice low but furious. Then with sudden insight, she added, 'Who was the woman who bruised your ego so much you decided never to trust one of us again?'

He gave a soft, unpleasant laugh. 'And *that's* typical of the way a woman's mind works! Any criticism of their kind has to be construed as the result of a love affair gone sour.'

But he hadn't denied it, she thought, staring into his face, and wondering how close her guess had come.

He looked back, his face enigmatic, faintly scornful. 'Tonguetied, Kerin? Or wondering what strategy to adopt next? What was it you wanted, anyway?'

She sighed in exasperation. 'Just to explain about the

dog,' she told him. 'I was foolish enough to think you might listen to reason. Why did you avoid me this afternoon?'

For a moment she thought he was going to deny it. Then he said, 'I thought I was about to be treated to a tearful plea for the pup's life. Was I wrong?'

'Yes. Even if I'd thought of it, I would never have imagined that tears would arouse any compassion in *you*.'

'You think me incapable of it? Don't you think I might have been avoiding you because I was afraid that I might yield to your entreaties?'

She looked at the cynical curve of his mouth, the mockery in his eyes, and said, 'No, I know you better than that. And I should have thought you would know *me* well enough by now not to expect any entreaties.'

'Don't you really care about the pup?' he asked abruptly.

'Of course I care!' she said passionately. 'But I realise there's nothing to be done about it. Have you been waiting for me to get hysterical about it? I'm sorry to disappoint you!'

'I'm not disappointed,' Dain said quietly, apparently answering her sarcasm quite seriously. 'They don't do, you know. Long-haired huskies have been known to injure themselves so badly they have to be destroyed in the end. It's better this way.'

'Yes, I know. Mitch explained.'

He touched her arm very fleetingly as he turned to go. Kerin wasn't sure if the soft words he murmured were really, 'I'm sorry!'

CHAPTER TEN

THE summer seemed to draw rapidly to its close, the heat of the low-dipping sun diminishing so that the personnel at the base and in the field more often wore their insulated mukluks and down clothing, and the winds that made even the sunniest day turn bone-chillingly cold seemed to have increased in frequency and knifelike power.

Beards turned into frost-rimed Santa-like whiskers in no time on the men who wore them, and a variety of strange devices were worn to protect faces from the cold and consequent frostbite. Some of the men had perspex visors that kept out the cold but tended to fog up, some wore close-fitting balaclavas, and others relied on a combination of woollen hats and scarves within their parka hoods. A few used bandages or nose-shields.

Kerin had rapidly decided she couldn't bear the feel of a balaclava which gave her a suffocating sensation, and used a long woollen scarf over her head and when necessary pulled across her face leaving only her eyes visible within the fur lining of her parka. Guy told her it gave her a mysterious Eastern look, and she retorted that his fantasy life was showing. 'Wishful thinking, my lad,' she grinned. 'I feel more like an Eskimo than a harem inmate.'

'*You're* the one who could have a harem here,' he said. 'In reverse. Hey, can I be your favourite?'

Kerin laughed. Guy was good fun in this mood, and indeed most of the time. He didn't handle alcohol very well, but he had not over-indulged since Christmas, and although Kerin was aware he would have liked to form a closer relationship with her, she successfully kept him at arm's length with a friendly firmness of manner that still left room for jokes like this.

Eddie was another who showed his admiration for her in

130

a frankly male way, but accepted her casual friendliness easily. He was an amateur painter, on fine days setting up an easel outside to try and capture the awesome beauty about them on canvas. Once or twice he had persuaded Kerin to appear in his painting, her parka hood pushed back as she obediently sat on a sled gazing at distant mountains or leaned against one of the huts to 'give it life', as Eddie explained. 'A picture with a girl in it always looks better,' he said firmly.

He had to fly out to Marie Byrd Land to pick up one of the last of the field parties who were coming into base ready for the trip home or the winter at the base. 'Come along for the ride,' he suggested. And Kerin accepted. She hadn't seen that particular camp, and she always accepted a new experience of the Antarctic when it offered.

He landed the helicopter on a snowfield near a rocky mountain peak, where their breath came short and fast and steamed in the cold air. The two men they picked up stacked their gear into the machine while Kerin took photographs of the surrounding snowfield and the commanding mountains that overshadowed it. Bare grim outcrops of grey and buff, they held the geological clues to the history of Antarctica, its relationship to the other continents to which it might have been joined aeons ago; and fossils showing a rich plant life it had once enjoyed before the ice claimed it for its own.

They took off in clear weather, the beating blades lifting them easily against a blue sky, but then clouds appeared seemingly out of nowhere and the sky became overcast. They merged with the white horizon in the distance and then the horizon disappeared altogether.

Eddie's lips were moving, he frowned and began to scan the ground below anxiously, and Kerin cast him a concerned glance. The far white horizon seemed to be closing in on them, and her fears were confirmed when Eddie shouted fiercely, obviously minding his language for her sake, 'It's a ruddy white-out!' And then, shaking his head and peering through the perspex in front of him, 'Where the hell is the ground?'

It was impossible now, to tell, for the sky and the snow-covered land seemed to have merged completely. It was like flying in a bowl of milk, with no landmarks and no sense of direction. Kerin suspected that even Eddie couldn't be certain the craft was still upright. A white-out, she knew, was the most dreaded of all conditions to Antarctic pilots. On the ground it was confusing and rather frightening, but one could stay still until it was over. Here, with the reflected sunlight glancing off the snow on to low cloud, then back to the snow until all shadow and contrast was removed by the glare, the effect was terrifying. Her teeth clenched tight with fear and her heart bumped irregularly.

Eddie cast a despairing glance upward and yelled, 'I'll try to get through the cloud!' and the machine began to ascend.

Kerin wondered if the three men were praying as hard as she was as the helicopter rose and swayed. Eddie was sweating, his hands showing white-knuckled on the controls, but the machine was still in the air, and she looked up, hoping for a break in the suffocating whiteness, a glimpse of blue sky.

But it didn't come. Instead there was a sudden, terrible jarring, a protesting scream of metal, and the machine lurched, stopped, turned slowly over and settled at a drunken angle against the slope of a mountainside, driving itself into the snow mantle.

Kerin found herself suspended by the webbing seat belt, her legs dangling. Eddie was half lying across the controls, his head bleeding a little, and one of the other men could be heard behind her cursing in a soft string of words.

Eddie stirred and wiped his head in a dazed way, then said, 'Let's get out of here, folks. She might go up.'

They helped each other out of the wrecked machine into the snow, keeping an eye out for any sign of fire. One of the geologists had a broken leg, that was obvious, and the other had dislocated his shoulder and breathed with difficulty, saying, with effort, that he thought he might have cracked a rib. Kerin had got off the most lightly, as the craft had tipped away from her, but some of the supply boxes in the rear had shifted and caused injuries to the two men back there with them.

They splinted the broken leg as best they could, and Eddie, with a muttered prayer of thanks that the radio was undamaged, began sending distress messages.

Eddie and Kerin pulled sleeping bags and groundsheets from the wreck and made the two injured as comfortable as possible before they set about putting up one of the colourful, insulated tents about them. It wasn't easy, but they thought it better not to move the injured men any more than absolutely necessary, and the small round entrance in the wall of a polar tent didn't give the easiest access in the world, even when the tube of fabric that kept it closed was tied back.

At last the white-out cleared and soon afterwards they heard the welcome sound of the base's other helicopter approaching, and began signalling until they were spotted and the machine hovered, descended and settled with great delicacy on the smooth snow.

Kerin was surprised to see a grim-faced Dain Ransome jump out and run crouching away from the propellers, before the pilot turned off the engine and alighted.

Blue eyes scanned her from head to foot and he demanded, 'Are you all right?'

'Yes,' she said. 'More all right than anybody.'

He turned to Eddie. 'Two injured, you said?'

'In the tent. We'll have to take it down again to get them out,' Eddie grinned. 'We'll have to take it down . . .'

'Okay, let's take a look.'

He inspected and approved the first aid, joked with the two men and said, 'Well, we'll get you into the other helicopter and then, I think, to McMurdo for a proper hospital going-over.'

'Have to take the tent down,' said Eddie, and Dain cast a

sharp glance at him, noting the thin trace of dark blood that emerged from his hairline on to his forehead.

'Got a bit of a bang on the head, did you, Eddie?' he asked.

'Gee, that's nothing, Dain. I'm okay.'

'Sure. Still, we'll send you along to McMurdo as well, just for a check-up. Kerin, too.'

'I'm perfectly all right,' Kerin protested. 'Not a scratch.'

Dain shrugged and didn't answer, turning his attention to dismantling the tent with the least inconvenience to the men inside it.

With the two badly injured men installed there wasn't a great deal of room left for other passengers. Dain said, 'I'll stay behind. You can fetch me later.'

And Kerin said, 'So will I.'

'No, you won't,' Dain informed her quietly. 'You're going in the chopper with the rest.'

'There's hardly any room——'

'You're not that big.' His smile was white and narrow.

'You can't stay without a partner,' she said. 'Basic survival, rule one.'

'Are you quoting the book at me?'

'Yes.'

The pilot, who had been watching them, interrupted, 'Why don't I leave Eddie behind and take Kerin?'

'Because Eddie has concussion,' said Kerin, getting a sharp glance from Dain. 'Probably,' she added cautiously to her amateur diagnosis.

'He has?' the pilot asked, startled. 'He said he was okay.'

'He isn't,' said Dain. 'So make sure he gets medical attention along with the other two, before you come back for us.'

It had been an easier victory than she had expected, but Kerin didn't meet Dain's eyes again until the helicopter was safely away, and then she kept her gaze carefully bland and neutral. His seemed equally expressionless.

'They'll be back quite soon, won't they?' she asked.

'If we're lucky,' he said. 'But don't count on it.'

'What do you mean?'

'The Antarctic is unpredictable in the extreme.'

'I know that,' she said a trifle impatiently. 'But that isn't all that you meant, is it?'

Dain looked about at lowering cloud and a blank white landscape. 'I think,' he said deliberately, 'there's a blizzard blowing up.'

It wasn't very long before Kerin discovered he was perfectly right, a circumstance that caused her some unreasonable irritation. They were still putting up the tent when the first gusts of gale-force winds hit them, and needle-sharp particles of dry, sandy blown snow stung at the exposed skin that her parka, glasses and scarf failed to cover. She silently railed at the clumsiness of heavy mittens as she pulled at flapping corners and manoeuvred boxes of supplies on to the tent flaps to hold them down on the snow, and was guiltily thankful when Dain shouted against the rising wind, 'You fix the inside!'

She wriggled through the tube at the entrance and began to roll out a mat for the floor, arrange the sleeping bags on their thin foam mattresses, and place the small kerosene cooker on an upturned box, with the opened emergency rations box in front of it.

It seemed a long time before Dain came in, and when he did, shaking snow off his clothing as he removed goggles, hood and gloves, Kerin asked more sharply than she intended, 'What have you been doing?'

'Fixing an outhouse,' he said evenly, giving her a sharp glance. 'We could be here for days. Can you light that thing?'

'Yes,' she said, finding the matches in the supply box and gingerly applying it to the burner. Automatically she held her chilled hands before the small flame for a few moments, and glanced up as Dain sat down on one of the sleeping bags. Her gaze stilled on his face and she exclaimed, 'Your face—frostbite!'

He cupped his hands in front of his face, breathing into

them, but still when he moved them and looked at her enquiringly, the white patch on his cheekbone remained visible.

Kerin moved and placed her warmed palm over the spot, feeling the coldness of it, and just below, the faint roughness of bristles.

Her gaze collided with a blue glance and she moved a little, crouched near him, almost overbalancing. A hard hand caught at her arm to steady her, and she said, 'Thank you.'

'Thank *you*,' he said. 'Is it working?'

She moved her hand and looked. 'It's beginning to.' She began rubbing it with her fingertips, needing some sort of action. 'Why don't you wear a beard?'

'To combat frostbite, you mean? It does help to a certain extent, but I found I hated the feel of an iced-up beard. I also hate the growing process—it itches.'

She moved her fingers, the tips lingering against his jawbone, and said, 'I think it's all right now.'

He caught her hand as it dropped from him, and said, 'Thanks.' Then he released her to sit back on her heels and turn from him, looking at the packets, tins and cooking utensils in the food box.

'Shall I cook tonight?' he asked.

'Would you? I do feel a bit—inadequate—with all this deyhdrated stuff.'

'That's the first time I've heard you admit to inadequacy,' he scoffed, quite gently. 'Are you sure you didn't hit your head, too?'

Surprised, Kerin glanced up at him, finding a gleam of genuine humour in his eyes. 'I told you,' she said, 'I was quite unhurt.'

'When did you realise that Eddie had concussion?'

'Not until after you came,' she confessed. 'He seemed quite normal until he started going on about taking down the tent.'

'Like a stuck record,' Dain murmured.

Kerin laughed a little, and then sobered. 'Will he be all

right? Concussion can be serious, can't it?'

'I'm not a doctor. I expect he'll be quite okay. They have a properly equipped hospital at McMurdo.' He paused, and although she kept her eyes on the blue flame of the burner she could feel his gaze on her face. 'Would you have been so calm if you realised that Eddie was injured as well?'

'Calm?' she queried.

'When we arrived you looked as calm as a nun, not at all like a girl who had been in a crash on a mountain at the bottom of the world.'

'What were you expecting?' she asked. 'Raving hysterics?'

'Not from you,' he said.

She looked back at him again, but the expression in his eyes was unreadable. He had seemed more friendly than usual since the others left, though. Lightly she said, 'Can I take that as a compliment?'

'Take it as you like,' said Dain. She thought his eyes were smiling. Then they alerted, suddenly. 'You're looking a bit seedy now though,' he commented, leaning closer. 'Sure you're feeling okay?'

'Yes,' she said, too quickly, and he slid off the sleeping bag and came to kneel beside her, taking her shoulders in his hands.

'You don't have to keep proving you're better than the next man,' he said roughly. 'What is it? Delayed shock?'

'I don't know,' she said. 'I'm all right if I keep still, honestly. But I didn't feel too good outside. My head ached terribly and I felt rather sick.'

A faint grin touched his mouth. 'Is *that* all?'

'All?' she repeated indignantly.

'We're pretty high up,' he said, the grin widening. 'The air is getting thin here. You have a touch of altitude sickness.'

'*Oh!* Oh, yes, of course.' She had read about it, but the reality had come as a surprise.

Dain made her take off her parka and windproofs and

crawl into her sleeping bag, after the briefest possible visit to the igloo-style outhouse he had dug in the snow a few yards from the tent.

Then she watched as he deftly melted snow, then mixed dried potatoes and dehydrated meat into more than palatable rissoles, and made pancakes with milk powder and dried egg powder.

She was more hungry than she realised, and felt better after the meal. He handed her an enamel mug full of strong coffee and as she took it, she said, 'I compliment the cook. My turn tomorrow.'

He didn't argue, and they sat quietly sipping their coffee while the blizzard raged and shrieked outside, shaking the walls of the tent so that the fabric trembled. But the little burner heated their small shelter remarkably efficiently, and Kerin felt quite cosy and safe, with Dain sitting only feet away on his own sleeping bag.

They wiped the dishes with paper and stowed them back into the box, and Kerin didn't even need to get out of the cosy down bag to do that. The tent was very small, the fifteen-inch insulating layer of air trapped between the inner and outer walls making it even less roomy than it looked from the outside.

'How do you feel now?' Dain asked as he adjusted the flame on the burner.

'Better, thank you.' She did, but she had suddenly become conscious of the intimacy of their situation. Crouched in the small space between the two sleeping bags, he looked calm and confident and rather too large and masculine. He had opened the collar of his thick plaid shirt and turned back the sleeves, and as he raised a hand to brush back a wayward strand of hair she saw the gleam of fine golden hairs on his strong forearm. His eyes met hers and she looked quickly away.

He opened his sleeping bag and slipped off his boots and one pair of socks and got inside the bag, leaning his head back on clasped hands.

'Care for a game of cards?' he asked, slanting a glance across at her.

She said, 'Do *you*?'

'Not particularly. But it's too early to sleep.'

'Yes. What do you usually do—in this situation?'

'Play cards, read—talk. Men in the Antarctic get to know each other quite well when they're tented up in a blizzard for a few days. Once cards and chess pall, and the reading matter runs out, there isn't much to do but talk.'

'What do they talk about?' she asked, quelling a faint excitement arising from the thought that she might get to know Dain Ransome better in this enforced isolation.

His faint grin laced with cynicism, he said, 'They talk a lot about women.'

Silent for a moment, she said with detached conviction, '*You* don't.'

He turned his head a little to look at her more fully. 'How would you know?'

Challenging him, Kerin looked back into the faintly mocking blue eyes. He wouldn't casually discuss a woman he cared for, she knew. And he was much too confident of his own masculinity to need to boast of unimportant conquests. 'You're not the type,' she said flatly.

He moved, and involuntarily she tensed, but he was only turning on his side, propping himself on one elbow. 'What *type* am I, then?' he asked her. 'Do you have me down as a woman-hater?'

She hesitated, a little alarmed because she had obviously needled him, even if only slightly, and she felt disadvantaged, flat on her back in the cocoon of the sleeping bag. But she wouldn't back down now. Across the small space that separated them she said, 'Not exactly. You look on women in much the same way you look on good wine or music— you appreciate and enjoy them when you have time for them, and provided they're kept in the small part of your life you can spare for them. You would never allow a woman to become important enough to influence your life.

She would have to take second place to your work.'

'How very astute of you, Kerin,' he said softly. 'You have me all worked out, don't you?'

'It's true, isn't it?'

'Basically,' he said shortly, and rolled back on to his hands again. 'Tell me about Roger.'

Taken aback, she said defensively, 'Why should I?'

'Why not? Isn't he the person who's most in your thoughts—the one you can't wait to get back to?'

'Of course,' she said. But a faint tide of dismay rose in her, because she realised that actually she had scarcely thought of Roger since his last letter. Life had been too full of other things—and people. 'But I don't want to bore you,' she added.

'Is Roger boring?'

'Of course not! He's a charming and talented and exciting person.'

'Exciting?' The blue eyes turned again to look piercingly at her. 'You mean sexually?'

'*No!*'

'Oh? He isn't?'

About to flare in temper, she checked herself. He was teasing her, of course, waiting for just that. 'I wasn't discussing that aspect,' she said coolly. 'And I'm not going to.'

'Don't you think "that aspect" is important in marriage?'

'I merely think it's private,' she said sharply.

His narrow smile held a certain insolent resignation. 'So you won't tell me if you sleep with him?'

'I certainly won't!' she snapped, outraged. 'If you want to satisfy your prurient male instincts, I suggest you find some of Eddie's magazines. I daresay he left some about.'

His jaw tightened, and the slight stain of colour on his cheekbones might have been anger. 'I told you, I don't go for that sort of stimulation.' But suddenly he moved, sitting up and twisting to look at her. 'Nor am I turned on by someone else's reminiscences. I prefer the real thing, at first hand.'

His hard gaze held a glitter that left her in no doubt what

he meant. Feeling disadvantaged, Kerin sat herself up, too. The bag slipped from her shoulders and she clutched it as it fell about her waist. 'If you mean what I think——' she said, and was stopped by the taunting quality of his smile.

'What do you think?' he asked.

She looked back at him in frustrated anger, fists tightly clenched on the billowing folds of her sleeping bag.

Dain suddenly laughed. 'You look like a Sabine maiden,' he said. 'Don't worry, I don't think a polar tent is a suitable venue for rape, even if I was tempted to it.'

'I'm not worried!' she said.

'On the grounds that I wouldn't do it, or that you can look after yourself?'

'Both.'

'Are you so sure?'

'Of the second, very. Of the first——' she hesitated fractionally. 'You just said yourself you're not tempted.'

'True.' He leaned forward suddenly, making her flinch, but he was only putting out the burner.

He looked up at her movement and said, 'It's better out while we sleep. There's a danger of carbon monoxide poisoning.'

'Yes,' she said, and wriggled down into the sleeping bag, pulling it round her chin, and adjusting the hooded top.

She turned her head away from him, but she could hear his even breathing, feel his presence in the slowly cooling tent, knowing that she need only stretch out her hand to touch him.

It seemed a very long time before she went to sleep.

When she woke hours later she found ice on her sleeping bag where her breath had condensed during her sleep, and beside her the tent wall had a thin coating of ice as well. But the burner was showing a feeble flame, and there was no sign of Dain. He must have lit it before going out.

There was a small amount of water left from the snow they had melted last night, and she dipped a facecloth and had a hasty wash and cleaned her teeth. She would offer to collect more herself to make up for the luxury of using precious water for washing.

'How's the weather?' she asked Dain when he crawled back into the tent.

'The same,' he answered laconically, pushing back his parka hood. 'Feeling better?'

'Yes, thanks,' she answered. She shrugged into her parka and windproofs and donned gloves and boots. 'I'll take a pot for water,' she said, and left him.

Outside the cold and the savagery of the hurled snow made made her gasp. She could barely see the outline of the igloo, and gathering a pot full of snow became a major task. The tent was already half buried in snow, and she wondered if it was possible it might be completely covered and never found . . .

She staggered back thankfully into the warmth of the tent, which now seemed like a sauna compared with the wild chill of the outside, their wet socks and mittens from yesterday steaming gently where they hung on a rope above the burner.

She placed the pot of snow on the burner and crouched in front of it for a few moments hugging herself. The soft buzz of Dain's battery-operated shaver stopped behind her and she asked, 'What would you like for breakfast?'

There wasn't a great deal of choice, really, but the potato omelettes she managed to turn out were at least passable with tomato sauce, and the hot coffee afterwards was comforting, too.

Once the dishes were done again there was nothing to do but crawl back into their sleeping bags, although later the temperature rose enough to bring them out, lying on top, or sitting crosslegged while Dain taught her how to play rummy. He was both patient and teasing, and Kerin felt more at ease than she ever had in his company.

He made them soup for lunch, and afterwards they sat talking quite companionably, when she asked him about his other Antarctic seasons, and what he knew of the parts she hadn't seen.

'The deserts,' he said. 'In Victoria Land. You've heard of the Dry Valleys?'

'Yes—there's no snow there.'

'That's right. About four thousand square miles of rocks and sand. It's a geologist's paradise. No ice, not even soil, to get between us and the earth's history. Although it's as contradictory as the rest of Antarctica. Lake Vanda is covered in a foot of ice, and at the bottom has a temperature of eighty degrees Fahrenheit. And Don Juan Pond never freezes although it's only six inches deep.'

'But why?'

Dain grinned. 'Salt. The water's full of it. Maybe left over from a time when the valleys were under the sea. There are mummified seals in the valleys, too, hundreds of years old, it's thought, and sixty miles inland.'

'Is it as beautiful as the rest of the continent?' Kerin asked.

'In its way. It's—aweful, in the ancient sense. Or awesome. There are tremendous vistas of glaciers spilling down into rocky valleys, mountain ranges that seem to climb endlessly into infinity, rocks and mountains sculpted by the wind into strange pyramid shapes. There are frozen waterfalls against grey rocky cliffs and icy lakes reflecting the brilliance of the sky on a blue, sunny day. And all kinds of oddly beautiful rock formations. And always the thrill of knowing that there are still discoveries to be made, that anything might turn up.'

'Like the giant salamander? It was found by a New Zealander, wasn't it?'

Dain smiled. 'That was the find of the century. A two-hundred-million-year-old fossil fragment showing that Antarctica had once been inhabited by some sort of reptile more than four feet long. The significance is, of course, that it was an inhabitant of semi-tropical forest areas.'

'And that means that the Antarctic was once much warmer.'

'That's right. Which supports the continental drift

theory, of course—that once the continent was much closer to the Equator.'

'Then perhaps those icebergs you talked about once before, drifting to warmer waters, are simply heading home.'

'Home? Icebergs have no home. They're wanderers on the face of the earth—or sea.'

'Do *you* have a home, Dain?'

He looked surprised. Kerin was surprised herself. The question had been quite unpremeditated, but she suddenly wanted very much to know the answer.

'Sort of,' he said. 'I own the family farm, since my parents died some years ago, within a year or two of each other. The place is run by a sharemilker, but I have a couple of rooms where I keep some stuff, mostly books and clothes. I don't have many possessions, as such. I move about too much to accumulate much.'

'A wanderer on the face of the earth?' she said softly, smiling.

His mouth quirked in reply, he inclined his head to her a trifle ironically. 'And you?' he asked. 'Do you have a home, parents, a family?'

'My father died when I was ten. My mother married again just seven years ago, and when I was twenty-one, she and her husband moved to Australia. They have another daughter, my half-sister. She's much younger than I am, of course.'

'Do you see them?'

'Not óften. We write. Once they holidayed here, and I've flown over in my holidays a few times. They make me very welcome.'

As a visitor, she was thinking. It was nobody's fault that she felt an outsider in their family circle, they were always very charming to her and her mother loved having her. But she was no part of their lives, just a pleasant diversion for a short time, someone to be entertained.

'Don't you get on with your stepfather?' Dain asked, watching her face.

'Of course I do! Only I don't think of him as that. I was

already an adult when he married my mother.'

'Just barely, surely. What is your mother like?'

'Small and sweet and very feminine.' She cast him a slightly mischievous glance and said, 'Not a bit like me!'

He grinned his acknowledgement. 'I wouldn't say that,' he murmured. 'Did you by any chance take it on yourself to look after your mother when your father died?'

'Nothing like that!' she said a little dryly. 'I said she was sweet and feminine, but it doesn't necessarily equate with "helpless", you know. I did have to do a certain amount of looking after myself, however. I'm glad of it, now. It made me independent and—capable, I think.'

'Capable of anything, I'd say.'

'Are you being nasty?'

'Why should you think that? Surely it's a compliment?'

'You tell me!'

'Okay,' he said easily. 'It's a compliment. Satisfied?'

Kerin laughed and said, 'Thank you.'

But when she stopped laughing something in his blue eyes made her catch her breath, and she looked away from him, her heart unaccountably thudding.

'What's the matter?' he asked, and it seemed to her that he knew, and that his voice was taunting, knowing.

'Nothing!' she said, too loudly. 'When is this blizzard going to *stop*?'

Of course he couldn't answer that, and he didn't try. He leaned across and his hand grasped her wrist, as he said questioningly, 'Kerin?'

She wasn't sure exactly what happened, only that his touch aroused a sudden fire that frightened her, so that she jerked away with unnecessary force, and pushed at him, saying fiercely, '*Leave me alone!*'

She caught him off balance, and he knocked hard against the little Primus stove, making her heart lurch in sickening fear as the flame flared suddenly, and instantly pictures danced in her head of the tent in flames and the two of them trapped inside it.

They both leaped to right the stove, knocking against

each other in their haste, and when it sat safely upright again, drawing back with arms entwined, clutching each other in relief. Dain was half kneeling, his thigh hard against Kerin's hip, his arms cradling her, fingers tight on her shoulder, her head against his as she curled her own fingers about the rough wool of his collar. She could feel the thud of his heart against her breast.

'You little fool!' he muttered, his voice deep and rasping.

'I'm sorry!' she whispered. 'Are you all right?'

'Yes.' He didn't ask her, but grasped her fingers in his and looked at the hand she had used to right the stove. She wasn't burnt—it had been too quick.

His fingers suddenly contracted on hers until his grip hurt, and she realised that she was trembling. Then he let go her hand and his long fingers cupped her cheek and chin, raising her face to his.

She knew he was going to kiss her, and her lips involuntarily parted a little as his mouth found them. It was a long, deeply satisfying kiss that seemed to draw a small, licking flame from the depths of her body. Her hand relaxed its death grip on his collar as he moved a little, fitting her head into the curve of his shoulder and arm, and her fingers touched the warm skin of his neck under his hair, slipped inside his shirt and softly stroked the muscles of his shoulder.

She thought his mouth was drawing softly away, but then he seemed to change his mind, to come back to her with renewed urgency, parting her lips again to ardent surrender, and, still kissing her, he moved and lowered her gently on to her sleeping bag, easing his body against the length of hers, moving his hand down the fine wool of her jersey, lingering on the feminine curves it covered and flooding her being with delicious longing.

Her own hands were restricted in their delicate exploration of his skin, and when the fabric of his shirt tautened and then a button gave way and freed them a little, she felt a little surge of triumph as her fingers moved down to his chest, delighting in the slightly damp warmth, the hard masculinity beneath the surprising smoothness.

Dain's hands moved convulsively, then, almost roughly pushing aside the constriction of her jersey, easily dealing with the fine cellular wool spencer she wore beneath that, beginning their own sure caresses of her bared midriff until he found the band of her bra and moved impatiently past that to find a strap and fumble that aside, too.

And Kerin came suddenly back to earth. Once Roger had been doing just that, when the sudden memory of Dain Ransome's face had intruded. Now it was Dain making love to her, and it seemed as though all along that was what she had wanted. But it was *wrong*!

She stiffened and wrenched her mouth away from his, taking in a sobbing breath. She felt confused and ashamed and frightened. She felt Dain's mouth against her throat and cried. '*No!* Stop it! Oh, stop!'

He lifted his head then, frowning as though he couldn't believe what he heard. 'What?' he said, and his voice sounded almost drugged.

She began to struggle and he suddenly grabbed her hair and made her keep still while he looked down into her face. She tightened her lips and whispered, 'Please, Dain. Let me go.'

He did, rolling away from her to his own side of the tent.

She touched her mouth that was tingling from his kisses, and sat up, keeping her eyes averted.

Almost indifferently, he asked, 'What happened? Did you suddenly remember Roger's existence?'

Too shaken to pretend or to think of some other excuse, she said dully, 'That's exactly what happened. I'm sorry if you're—disappointed. But you——'

'I what?'

'You shouldn't have kissed me.'

Into the deadly little silence that followed, he said, 'I thought I received a definite invitation.'

That was beastly, and she looked up then, anger in her

eyes, to find him looking maddeningly calm, with his cynical smile well in place. He said, 'No?' and raised an eyebrow.

'No.'

He shrugged contemptuously, as though he didn't believe her but it was too unimportant to argue anyway. Her anger grew into a hard knot of resentment, but she swallowed it down.

The tent seemed stiflingly small and stuffy, and she looked in some despair at the flimsy walls that made such an effective prison in the midst of the blizzard . . .

And then she realised that the blizzard had died. The tent fabric hung still at last, and there was no muted howling going on outside.

She looked about, listening, and it was true. Dain was watching her, and she met his eyes and said, 'It's stopped . . . hasn't it?'

'Yes. Some time ago. If it lasts, they'll be out to pick us up quite soon.'

Kerin swallowed, surprised by a quite extraordinary rush of contradictory feelings—relief and a sudden release of tension, and impatience to be gone from here, but shot through with opposing emotions of regret and depression.

'Will Roger be waiting for you?' Dain asked suddenly. 'When you get back to Christchurch?'

'Yes,' she said, 'I certainly hope so.'

Softly he taunted, 'What will you tell him?'

She drew in a sharp breath and said, 'It's none of your business what I tell him.'

'Oh, I think I might be called an interested third party,' he drawled. 'Supposing *I* decided to tell him how sweetly his fiancée makes love in an Arctic tent, when the mood takes her . . .'

She turned on him in fury. 'You swine! If you . . .'

'*Don't* dare me!' he warned her, his voice cutting like a knife into her protest.

She breathed deeply, unevenly. 'Sometimes,' she said, 'I hate you more than any man on earth!'

'Only sometimes?' He laughed, and said, stirring from

his position, 'I'll go and check the weather, and see if the radio can get through.'

Kerin didn't watch him go out, sitting with her knees up and her hands clasped in front of her. She was trying to tell herself that what she had said to him was true, that she really did hate him. But the anger in her was at war with another bewildering new emotion that she didn't want to recognise or admit. She couldn't—she couldn't have possibly been stupid enough, she told herself, to fall in love with a man of ice!

CHAPTER ELEVEN

By the end of March the last of the summer people had left, the buildings had been checked and sealed about the doors and windows with wide cloth tape, and the chimneys covered. The tracks to the water source and the met. box where daily weather readings had to be made were marked with six-foot poles and red flags in expectation of the deep winter snows to come. Seabirds no longer wheeled about the coast and flocked on the offshore floes, and the penguins had moved from the nesting sites out to the floating ice at sea.

The sun moved lower towards the horizon and nights became long. Sometimes the sun surrounded itself with mysterious rings and rays or flung an image of itself on to the ice crystals suspended in the air so that it appeared twice, or the image hung in the sky while the original hid beyond the horizon. Already there was darkness at midnight for a couple of hours.

The dozen people left at the base seemed to draw closer to one another as the length of the nights increased until the sun dropped from sight for the last time and the flags were lowered for the long Antarctic night.

Except for Dain, who appeared to Kerin to become more aloof and unapproachable as the temperature dropped and the winter closed in. She watched the men and noted their reactions, the ones who complained that they couldn't sleep when night never lifted—sometimes the same men who had been sleepless in the nightless summer months, the ones who seemed to withdraw into their work or hobbies and spent most of their time alone, the ones who became irritable or teased each other with an edge of malice, and the few who slept most of the time.

But Dain Ransome's reactions remained unfathomable.

He was quietly watchful, once or twice authoritative when irritation threatened to become anger, incisively cutting into arguments before they became fights, cooling down the participants with a few well chosen words. He never showed the least anger or irritability himself, and Kerin tried to laugh at herself when she realised that she was finding *that* intensely irritating.

She was aware that to most of the men she had become some sort of special symbol. No one ever turned their frustrations on her. There seemed a sort of tacit conspiracy to protect her from their less amiable moods, and she noticed that she was getting the 'lady treatment' as she labelled it privately, intrigued by this particular phenomenon, and rather amused at her own instinctive reaction. Men opened doors for her, served her first, watched their language with exquisite delicacy when she was about, and asked for her 'woman's viewpoint' on all sorts of discussions during the evening sessions of talk and drinking.

She had become for them, she deduced, a substitute for all the women they had left behind and hoped to return to, a focus for their tenderness and chivalry, and surely there wasn't a woman alive who would not have become more aware of her own feminine nature under this subtle flattery. She found herself developing an almost maternal affection for them all, and was often the recipient of their confidential hopes and longings, particularly those connected with their wives and girl-friends.

It became quite common for one or other of the men to sit with Kerin in a quiet corner of the mess for half an hour or so, and talk. And there seemed an unspoken agreement among the men that such tête-à-têtes were not to be disturbed.

She knew that Dain had become aware of the practice, and that he seemed to view it with some derision. Once he came over to her with a fresh drink in his hand for her, unrequested, after one of the men had just left her.

He took the man's place beside her and eyed her with a taunt in his smile. 'Playing Mother Confessor?' he asked.

'Or making mental notes for your report to Professor Prince?'

Kerin sipped at the drink and tried to quell a quick rush of anger. She never made notes, mental or otherwise, on these private conversations, and the substance of them would never appear, except in the most general terms, in her reports.

'I'm just being normally sociable,' she said.

His glance told her he didn't believe that. 'All these quiet, cosy conversations,' he said, his voice scoffing. 'What do they talk about? Let me guess. You remind them of the girl they left behind—is that it? They've made you a kind of mascot—a surrogate for all the girls they dream about in the long, cold night. They've endowed you with every feminine virtue, and all those poor girls back home are going to have to measure up to the goddess who wintered on the ice with them.'

There was some truth in what he was saying, she knew. But the way he said it antagonised her. Wanting to hit back, she snapped, 'And who do I remind *you* of, Mr Ransome? The girl who once cracked that lump of ice you call a heart—and made you hate her?'

She saw the flare of surprise in his eyes before he hid it behind a cold mask of indifference. But there was a vicious undertone in the coldness of his voice when he replied, 'Go and stick your pins in someone else, Miss Clever. I'm not in the market for psychoanalysis.' He put down his drink abruptly and stood up. 'I'm going for a run with a dog team.'

She said, 'Can I come?' not even thinking about it, but suddenly immensely attracted by the idea of sledging across immensity of ice in the bright cold moonlight.

Then she waited cringing for Dain's rebuff, because of course he didn't want her along. He wanted to get away from her.

But he stopped and looked at her, then said, 'If you like. Go and get some warm clothes. It's past twenty below, outside.'

She almost ran to do it, half afraid he would go without her if she didn't hurry, and strangely exhilarated by the thought of leaving the heat and confinement of buildings.

He was waiting for her when she stepped outside, and the chill struck at her face and sucked into her lungs with her first gasping breath. She pulled the woollen scarf about her face as they trudged towards the dog lines, telling herself she was quite mad, but feeling with every step an increase in the excitement that gripped her.

The dogs were excited, too, yelping and pulling on their chains as Dain unwound the rope traces from the sledge and handed the lead trace to Kerin, who stretched it out in front of the sledge while Dain anchored the back with a steel pin. Then she stood by the lead dog to hold the attention of the rest while Dain harnessed them. This few minutes was a time of tension, when fights might break out among the dogs, but it went without a hitch, and Dain said quietly, 'I'll brake,' as Kerin prepared to jump on and take the traces as the sledge passed her when the dogs began to pull.

It was an absolutely unforgettable experience, driving across the ice shelf in brilliant silver moonlight, the vast emptiness matched by a deep silence in which the soft padding of the huskies' feet, their panting breath, the swish of the runners gliding on the snow were the only sounds. Once they were on smooth flat snow, Dain moved from the back of the sled to sit just behind her, and they seemed to go on and on as though the dogs could carry them for ever into a magic Never-never-land.

The yellow flicker in the sky that came and went, then shimmered into life and disappeared, sent a tremor of expectant wonder down Kerin's spine, and she was already pulling on the traces before Dain's gloved hands reached round her to grasp them and his voice quietly called the team to a halt.

The dogs hunched down on to the snow, scooping up some with their tongues, and settling quietly, while Kerin leaned against the padded clothing that covered Dain's chest and said on a breath of sound, 'What is it?'

'Wait,' he said.

His arms tightened about her, and she huddled close, because it was very cold.

And then it began. The yellow glow appeared again, wavered in the sky, and grew stronger. It hovered, spread, stretched and seemed to fold like a curtain hung against the midnight sky. A green glow appeared at its edge, then there were suddenly bands of red, white, deep green, and violet chasing each other across the sky, until they merged and a glow of pink suffused the horizon on every side. A brilliant flash of light shot across from horizon to horizon and sometimes the entire sky seemed to be a moving mass of light and colour, an incredible display of awesome proportions, the pinks and purples and golds and crimsons mingling, separating, merging, hurling themselves across the heavens, then delicately hovering with a shimmering grace in ethereal, wavering curtains of light.

Kerin couldn't have said how long it lasted—minutes or hours. It was totally magic, taken out of time, an everlasting moment.

When at last the lights faded and the sky returned to blankness, they sat on for a few minutes in total silence. Then Dain stirred, and called the dogs to their feet, and they turned the team and returned to base. Any further exploration that night would have been anti-climactic.

Each dog received the regulation rewarding pat and approving words and then they walked back to the buildings, still wordless, but Dain's arm was about Kerin's shoulder, and it felt absolutely right.

When they reached the buildings, she said, 'Thank you for letting me come. Goodnight.'

He opened the door that led to her quarters before he answered. 'Goodnight, Kerin.' His voice sounded friendly and gentle, but he had already swung away before she got the heavy door closed.

Midwinter Day was a highlight of the Antarctic calendar. The cook excelled himself with scallops, oysters, turkey, and light fruit pies with ice cream, and the subsequent party went on for hours. An air of affectionate camaraderie prevailed and there were no tense incidents to mar the celebration.

The following days seemed flat, and some of the men became positively morose. Kerin noted that fact for Professor Prince, and did her best to remain calm and cheerful, and went out of her way to talk to the ones who seemed least communicative.

Eddie asked her to let him try a portrait of her, and was so disappointed at her initial laughing refusal that she relented and changed her mind. Small disappointments and frustrations took on unrealistic proportions in the unnaturally closed community, and she didn't want to be the cause of plunging poor Eddie into a gloom that was foreign to his normally happy nature.

She told herself that her own deep disappointment that Dain's manner had not changed since their sharing of the Aurora that night was due to the same cause. In normal conditions she would not have experienced this piercing hurt each time his cool eyes met hers with not a spark of warmth, with no apparent memory of shared moments of magic.

He was the only one who took no apparent interest in the picture Eddie was painting of her. There was no chance of keeping the sittings a secret, for if the two of them had disappeared for an hour or two at a time, in the abnormal conditions of the base rumour and speculation would have been rife, with a subsequently explosive situation.

When it was finished, it was a good amateur portrait, a little wooden but like her, and Eddie proudly hung it in the mess where everyone duly admired it.

Even Dain, pressed to give an opinion, said with a cool smile that he was impressed with Eddie's talent. When he moved his glance from the painting to her face and back, Kerin wondered if he thought Eddie had flattered her.

Someone said, 'How about painting something to go over the bar, Eddie?' and thrusting forward an art book he had been glancing through, added, 'Something like this?'

This, Kerin saw as she looked with others at the full colour plate, was *The Naked Maja*.

There were some goodnatured whistles and humorously enthusiastic encouragement, and Eddie, grinning, said, 'Think I couldn't, huh?' to those who sounded sceptical of his talents. 'Well, I'll show you bas—— Sorry, Kerin!'

She smiled forgiveness and said, 'That's right, Eddie, you show them!'

Later he came up to her quietly, holding the book in his hands, and said, 'You won't mind, Kerin? If I paint a nude for the boys? I mean, it won't be like——'

'Like what was there before?' she smiled.

Sheer horror crossed his pleasant face. 'You saw it?'

Kerin laughed and reassured him, 'No. Someone took it down before I had the chance.'

'Well,' said Eddie, looking very relieved, 'this will be something in watcha call good taste. I mean, I'm no great artist, I know that, but there's art and there's dirt, see, isn't there? That's the difference, I guess.'

'I'm sure yours will be art,' she smiled. She knew what he meant, although she supposed there was some difficulty about drawing the line. *The Naked Maja* might be a famous painting and classical enough to have gained respectability, but the lady had an undoubtedly erotic air, and she seemed to have read somewhere that the painting had caused a stir when Goya created it in 1800.

This time Eddie worked on the painting in his own room, answering all bantering queries as to the progress of it with the stolid information that they'd see when it was finished.

Kerin's birthday was in coldest mid-July. There had been no mail for months. Roger had sent a small parcel with the last batch of mail they had received, and she opened it that morning to find a pair of pearl drop earrings that looked elegant and expensive, and a card with Roger's equally elegant scrawl sending her his love.

The earrings were lovely, and the sentiment warm, and

she was a little horrified at herself because the only emotion she felt as she took the cold hard droplets in her hand was a vaguely defined depression and unease.

Of course it didn't mean anything, she told herself sensibly. It was ages since she had seen him, and the depression simply meant that she was missing him, that was all.

She didn't wear the earrings, but placed them back in their little box and put them away.

When Dain stopped by her table at lunch and put his tray down between hers and Nat Mitchell's, she glanced up in surprise. He must want to talk to Mitch, she supposed, but that impression was dispelled when before even sitting down, he said in a clear voice that half of the room at least must have heard, 'Many happy returns, Kerin.'

Surprised, she asked, 'How did you know it's my birthday?'

'It's in your file,' he told her, seating himself as congratulations from the other men flowed across the room, and someone started a chorus of Happy Birthday to You. Dain even joined in, his green eyes gleaming enigmatically, and when someone said, 'She should have a birthday party!' he endorsed the remark, with 'Good idea! We'll talk to the cook.' He smiled down at her and then turned his attention to his meal.

They gave her a party complete with hastily baked and iced birthday cake and champagne. And Dain stayed close to her all evening and proposed a toast for her birthday, and even suggested dancing.

He claimed the first dance from her himself, and as they circled the floor she asked, 'Why did you set this up?'

'What do you mean?'

She flashed him a glance and said, 'I'm not stupid! You knew someone would suggest a party as soon as they knew it was my birthday.'

'You're not stupid,' he acknowledged. 'Didn't you want a party?'

She hadn't cared, one way or the other. If he had wanted to give her a party, she thought she might have been pleased if he had suggested it outright, himself. But she couldn't help suspecting that his motives had been something more complex than a simple desire to give her pleasure. And that his methods had been somehow devious. Why had he waited for someone else to make the suggestion, having given them the obvious cue?

'That doesn't answer my question,' she said.

'Persistent little cuss, aren't you? All right, I wanted an excuse for a morale-boosting exercise. The men need it at this time of the year. We can't celebrate everybody's birthday, but yours, as you're the only woman and it's at the right time, made a perfect excuse. And it was better if it seemed a spontaneous gesture of the men, rather than the commander's treat.'

She swallowed. 'I see. And you're even allowing dancing. That's quite a concession, isn't it?'

His fingers tightened a little on hers. 'There are only a dozen of us now for you to distribute your favours around. Just make sure you dance with everyone and there'll be no problems.'

'Certainly, Commander,' she said with exaggerated compliance. 'In order of precedence?'

His eyes glinted as he looked down at her faintly flushed face and eyes bright with temper. 'That won't be necessary,' he drawled. 'I'd advise you to give young Guy a whirl before he gets himself too drunk to stand straight. After that, just remember the basic principle. Pat one, pat them all.'

'You think that people can be controlled in the same way as your dog teams?'

'This is a primitive environment, where men live close to nature and ancient instincts tend to come to the fore. They're only a little more complicated than the dog teams, that's all.'

'Does that include yourself?'

'My instincts are as powerful as any other man's. I've had some practice at keeping them well under control, however.'

'And now you're using me to control the others.'

'I'm using the fact that it happens to be your birthday.'

'Oh, don't hedge! You know very well you've done your damnedest to keep them from getting close to me. And now, because you feel it's time they had some—some light relief, some small reward for being good, you arrange dancing, and *instruct* me in my role. Every man gets his share, his turn to chew the bone!'

There was a tightness about his mouth, and his fingers hardened on her waist, as though they might bruise the flesh beneath her thin jersey. '*Be quiet!*' he muttered sharply, beneath his breath.

'Why don't you just say, "Heel!"' she asked him. 'It would do as well, wouldn't it?'

'Don't push me, Kerin,' he said softly, between shut teeth. 'I could be tempted to bring you to heel in a way you'd never forget!'

'Charming!' she said, giving him a totally insincere smile as the music stopped and she made to move out of his arms. As he still held her, she said quite gently, 'I've done my duty dance, Commander. Do you mind if I choose my own partner for the next one?'

He knew she was threatening not to obey instructions, but he had to let her go because the other men were gathering round now, vying for her. She did what she would have done anyway, and danced with them all, trying to ignore the cold blue eyes that followed her, ticking off the names, she was sure, on a mental list.

When Guy danced with her, holding her too close and whispering audacious compliments in her ear, she was tempted to play up to him, simply to give Dain Ransome something to think about, but she knew to show any favouritism would be unfair to everyone, including Guy.

So she warded him off, chiding him lightly, and when the music stopped turned with relief to the next man in line. Guy took it with good grace, but later in the evening was more belligerent when she refused to dance with him again. Again, the men united to protect her, and Guy found himself being half carried off to the other side of the room by a jovial Les and Mitch, while the golden-bearded young Sebastian swept Kerin over to the bar for another drink. And when she finished it she found Dain at her elbow and said lightly, looking boldly at his cold expression, 'Don't tell me, Commander—you're sending me off to bed—right?'

'I'll see you to your quarters,' he said levelly.

'Why, thank you, Commander!' she said in the same light tone as before, and called goodnight to the others as he took her arm in a firm grip and led her away from the bar.

They went through the covered ways, which took longer, but the outside temperature had dropped so far that a cup of boiling water flung into the air would freeze with a crackle before it hit the ground. It was no weather for walking outside, in the clothes the heating allowed them to wear in the mess. Even the covered ways were freezing, and they hurried through them without speaking, arriving at last in the cold-porch of the building housing Kerin's room, where she turned to Dain and said, 'I hope I satisfied your requirements?'

'You handled yourself very well.'

Surprised by the praise, but unwilling to relinquish easily her hurt anger, she said, 'Thank you. Is that by way of being *my* pat on the head—for being a good girl and letting you use me to keep the men happy?'

He opened the heavy door into the narrow heated passageway outside her room, and pushed her into it ahead of him, clanging the door shut and locking them in together.

She turned to face him defiantly, as he switched on the light, and she blinked into narrowed, glittering blue eyes.

'I told you,' he said, 'I wasn't trying to *use* you!'

'Weren't you? Then what was all that about distributing my favours equally?'

'That was just plain common sense——'

'Oh? Then why not credit *me* with some?' she asked.

'I'm really not the idiot you seem to think.'

'I've never thought that!'

Her eyes widened a little. 'Goodness me! The compliments are flowing thick and fast tonight. Are you quite yourself, Mr Ransome?'

A faint gleam of humour appeared in his eyes but quickly vanished. 'I wouldn't be too quick to call it a compliment,' he said a trifle grimly.

She kept looking up at him, working that out, remembering some of their past conversations. 'You think I'm some sort of scheming female,' she said at last.

'Just a female,' he corrected.

She took a quick breath, and said, 'I see. And you call yourself a scientist!'

On that scornful note, she turned to enter her little room, but an arm shot out and blocked her way, his hand flattened against the wall, so that she straightened against it herself to look at him. He was too disturbingly close like that, but her indignant stare failed to move him.

He demanded, 'What's that supposed to mean?'

'Can't you work it out?'

'Lost your nerve?'

She wouldn't let him think *that*! 'You don't frighten me!' she said.

'I could.' He didn't move, or raise his voice, but a shiver of apprehension moved down her spine. She tilted her chin defiantly to counteract it, and said, 'I meant—scientists are supposed to act on evidence, not prejudice.'

'And you think I don't?'

'Not as far as women are concerned.'

'But then you don't know what evidence I have to act on, do you?'

'If you mean your experience of women, I can guess it's been—unfortunate.' She kept her eyes on his, a kind of challenge.

'Oh, not entirely,' he said with soft meaning. 'But in my experience, women and the Antarctic don't mix. They draw the men's attention from their work, and then they can't resist playing off one man against another.'

'Is that what happened to you?' Kerin dared to ask, softly.

His gaze sharpened into steely mockery. 'Probing again? I told you not to stick your pins in me. You'd like to find a thwarted love in my past to account for my attitude to having women here, wouldn't you? But it isn't quite as simple as that. I've seen the pattern repeated often enough not to want to see it develop when I'm in charge. The simplest way to prevent it is not to have any women. The next best thing is to keep a damn good eye on——'

'*Me?*' She knew why he stayed so close to her whenever there was a party, why he watched her so much. He didn't trust her. 'I'm *not* like that!'

'I can't afford to take chances on it.'

'Doesn't it occur to you that if I was inclined that way, you couldn't stop me?'

'Don't count on it!'

Frustrated and nettled, she was in the mood to rise to any challenge.

'Supposing I decided to take you up on that!' she said. 'What could you do?'

Calmly Dain answered, 'I'd appropriate you myself. None of the men would meddle with my woman.'

'*Your*——' She almost choked with rage at his cool insolence. 'Aren't you forgetting—*that* would require a certain amount of co-operation from me?'

He didn't answer, but a second before he moved closer, pinning her to the wall with the hardness of his body, she stiffened and put up a hand to ward him off.

It didn't do any good. He captured her wrist in one hand and with the other under her chin forced her to meet his kiss. It was devastating, insolently sure and sensual.

Her free hand closed about his wrist, trying to pull his hand away from her face, and he turned it and captured her wrist instead. But when she tried to wrench her mouth away, she couldn't. His lips hardened, pressing her soft inner lip against her teeth until it hurt, and she gave a little muffled moan of protest.

He forced her wrists down to her sides against the wall, then shifted his position quickly, sliding an arm about her body that imprisoned hers, and pulled her close against him, while his other hand slipped under her hair and cradled her head, holding it at just the angle that he wanted as his mouth softened at last and began a soft, coaxing exploration that drew a dizzy spiral of excitement from somewhere deep within her body, a slow, sweet torment of desire that eventually she could hide no longer. A long, shuddering sigh brought her mouth sweetly open under his, and she let her body at last relax against the strength of his hands as they held her.

He moved again, shifting their feet a little, and with a gentle, insistent tug at her hair, lifted her head back while his lips slid warmly on to her arched throat, and his tongue found the hollow at its base. His hand came up to push aside the soft wool at her neckline and give him freer access to her smooth skin, and as he freed her hands she found herself holding him, her fingers spread on his back to bring him even closer.

His lips moved to just below her ear, and she heard him murmur her name, and fleetingly opened her eyes, realising dimly that he had moved them into her room. A faint tremor of warning fluttered in her throat, then suddenly he was withdrawing from her, his hands on her shoulders, the heat of his thighs against hers removed.

Kerin opened dazed eyes and fixed them on his mouth. It was smiling faintly, its hard outline softened. But when she met his eyes she found the passion fading from them into mockery, as they flickered over her, and her heated body suddenly chilled.

He didn't say a thing, but he didn't need to. The contemptuous triumph in the look he sent her as he turned toward the door said it all for him. The co-operation she had thought she could withhold was no longer in any doubt. He was very sure he would have got it.

CHAPTER TWELVE

ONE of the ways in which the long winter was consciously made less tedious for the base staff was the organisation of classes in various skills and lectures by the scientists about their own fields of expertise. When Dain gave a lecture on the geological history of the area Kerin found herself fighting inwardly against falling under the spell of his voice, and afterwards she left the mess abruptly while he was still answering questions.

She had hoped he wouldn't notice, but the next day as she stood making herself a drink of hot cocoa at the sideboard she found him beside her.

'Did I bore you last night?' he asked, pulling the top off a can of fruit drink.

'Not especially,' she said. 'I was tired.'

He gave her a sharp look and asked, 'Are you sleeping all right?'

'Yes.' She knew she had been looking a little drawn lately. And the cause was him. She found it a strain keeping out of his way, a feat that was practically impossible anyway, and more of a strain trying to act normally with him. She alternated between wanting to throw something at his indifferent head, and fighting a crazy desire to touch him and make him notice her. She told herself it was their abnormal living conditions that caused these intense emotions, that whatever she felt about Dain would fade when she returned home. Someone had said that in the winter-overs, everyone became slightly paranoid. She just wished her particular midwinter madness had taken another form than a hopeless infatuation for Dain Ransome.

Because that must be all it was, she told herself frantically. Dain Ransome wanted no ties with any woman, his heart belonged to his work. And she had Roger waiting for

164

her back home, waiting to give her a wedding ring to go with the engagement ring he had pressed on her before she left. Roger loved her. There wasn't a hope in the world that Dain Ransome ever would. He might enjoy kissing her occasionally, but she was no one special in his life. And even his kisses had been nearly always at least partly some kind of tactical move in the skirmishes that seemed inevitable between them. He knew very well that his lovemaking affected her—she hadn't been able to hide that. But she hoped he didn't realise how deeply.

She moved away from the sideboard with her cup and tensed when he followed her and sat opposite when she chose a chair at one of the tables.

'Think you'll last the winter?' he asked conversationally.

'I'll have to, won't I? Like everyone else.'

'Someone once said it's like going to war. Once you're in there's no turning back. You go forward or you go down.'

She raised her eyes to look at him. His looked watchful and interested. 'I won't go down,' she said, as if he had suggested she might.

'No,' he said slowly, 'I don't think you will.'

'Someone else said, didn't they, that everyone gets to know more about themselves?'

'I don't recall that, but I daresay it's true.'

'You've wintered over several times, haven't you?'

'Yes. Are you implying I ought to know myself rather well?'

'I'm implying you might know if what that person said was true.'

'I could only speak for myself.' The man of ice, not giving anything away.

Exasperated, Kerin refused to ask the next obvious question, and there was a short silence during which Eddie joined them with a brimming glass of beer.

'You look pleased about something,' Kerin told him, glad to be able to talk to someone else.

'Secret,' he grinned at her. 'Wanted to talk to you about it, Dain, if you've got a minute?'

Kerin rose. 'I know when I'm not wanted,' she shrugged.

'You know I didn't mean that!' Eddie protested. 'Finish your drink. I don't want to talk here, anyway.'

Kerin laughed and sat down. Suddenly anxious, Eddie asked, 'I didn't interrupt anything, did I?'

'Between us?' Dain smiled as though the idea was slightly ridiculous. 'Kerin had enough of my exclusive company out on the mountain after you crashed that chopper.'

'And the commander had enough of mine!' Kerin rejoined lightly.

'That I don't *believe*!' said Eddie with ponderous chivalry. 'The rest of us were green with envy at the time.'

'*You* were green, all right,' she laughed. 'But not with envy. Though I must admit I wouldn't have realised you were concussed if you hadn't kept repeating yourself.'

Ruefully, Eddie touched the small scar that still showed on his forehead. 'Well, that was nothing!' he said. 'A few days under observation and I was right as rain again. I still think I needn't have gone to McMurdo.'

'It could have been serious,' Dain said quietly. 'No more headaches lately?'

'Nope. Not for weeks. I told the medicos there was no need to wory about them. I'm as tough as old leather.'

'No doubt,' Dain smiled. 'But they weren't too happy about letting you come back to us so soon. I promised to keep an eye on you.'

Kerin finished her cocoa and left to go to her own room, saying lightly, 'I'll leave you to your secrets, then.'

About half an hour later she was sitting at her typewriter when a thunderous knock startled her.

She had hardly time to call 'Come in!' and swivel about in her chair when Dain flung open the door and slammed it shut behind him. He had an open parka flung over a dark, fitting sweater and dark pants, and he looked big, bulky and dangerous. The impression was heightened as he took a step into the small room and stopped with his feet apart and his

hands planted on his lean hips. Kerin rose to her feet, but
he still seemed to tower over her. In his compressed lips
and leaping eyes she saw a barely controlled rage.

'What on earth——?' she began.

But he gave her no chance to finish her bewildered question. In a furious, rigidly reined in voice, he said, 'Did
you know what Eddie was doing?'

'What are you talking about?'

'The painting Eddie's doing for the mess! He says you
knew what he was doing.'

'Well, yes, I knew.'

'You posed for him?'

Bewildered, she said, 'Yes, of course.' Everyone knew
she had posed for the portrait Eddie had done. 'You knew
that!'

Dain took a quick breath, then seemed to suddenly pull
himself up. 'Just a minute. You're talking about the portrait
of you?'

'Yes.'

'What about the new one that he's painting for the bar?
He said he asked you about the subject, and you okayed
it.'

'Well, yes, he asked my opinion.' But surely he didn't
think she'd posed for *that*!

'Then you know what the subject is?' he queried with
apparent sarcasm.

'Yes, I think so. It's a nude, isn't it?'

'It is. With your face.'

She should have known, she thought, that it was coming.
But she stood and looked at him in stunned silence, her lips
parted in shock, then she felt the heat of the flush that rose
to her cheeks.

As he watched her, the anger drained out of Dain's face.
He said flatly, 'You didn't know.'

Kerin swallowed, feeling dizzy. 'No.'

Had he really thought she did? She looked at his face,
trying to understand that he might have thought she
would be so foolish and so—so vulgar.

As though reading her thoughts, he said almost gently, 'He told me you'd given your permission.'

She shook her head. 'I just don't understand. He surely couldn't have thought——'

'He did. It's as well he thought I'd better see it before he put it up in the mess on public view.'

'What—what did you say to him?' she asked.

'Not much. What there was was short and to the point. He paints out that face tonight.'

'Thank you,' she whispered. 'I don't remember exactly what he said, but I understood he meant it to be a sort of interpretation of Goya's *Naked Maja*. He must have misunderstood—or *I* did.'

'Obviously. Next time be sure you know what you're saying yes to, will you?'

Was he blaming her? Shock and embarrassment receding a little, she lifted her head and said, 'I still can't believe that's what he meant! It isn't *like* Eddie!'

Dain looked derisive. 'He's a man, isn't he? And you know very well the kind of—literature—his taste runs to. What did you expect?'

'Not this, obviously!' she flashed.

'I see you've recovered your equilibrium,' he drawled, and pulled open the door.

Kerin watched him to turn to go, but he stopped when she said clearly, 'No! Dain—please wait!'

He stopped in the doorway and looked round at her enquiringly.

She said, 'It *isn't* like him! No—please!' she repeated as she caught the look of impatient disbelief on his face. 'It's something that's difficult to explain, but Eddie wouldn't normally dream of doing a thing like that—and he knows perfectly well I wouldn't agree to it if he suggested it. Laugh if you like, but he respects me—under all that brashness and kidding, he's a gentleman.'

His eyebrows rose at that, and he turned to face her fully, but he didn't laugh.

'He probably thought of it as a compliment to you,' he shrugged.

'I'm sure he did. But in a normal frame of mind he would have known it was a compliment I wouldn't welcome.'

His glance sharpened then. 'Are you suggesting a touch of midwinter madness, or something more?'

'Perhaps it's that. But he did have that concussion. I don't know much about it, but I believe a blow on the head can have serious repercussions for some time—cause people to act strangely, even seem to change their personalities.'

'*Lord!*' he exclaimed, and for the first time since she had known him, she saw his face assume a harassed expression. 'That's all I need!' he went on disgustedly.

'I may be wrong,' Kerin added.

'And you *may* be right,' he said broodingly, his eyes on her face, almost as though it was her fault. '*Damn!* If I was sure I'd ask them to risk sending a Hercules in for him. It has been done, but only in genuine emergencies.'

'Do you think it's necessary?'

He snapped, 'That's just what I don't know, isn't it!' Kerin blinked and he said shortly, 'Sorry. It's my problem.'

'If I could help . . .' She suddenly realised the enormity of the responsibilities that he carried, where he must decide things like this for all of them, cut off from the normal facilities taken for granted in civilised communities—the doctor on call, the hospital in town, the ready availability of transport routes and services.

'You can keep an eye on him,' said Dain. 'And tell me if anything else in his behaviour strikes you as unusual.'

Unable to resist the opportunity, she said dryly, 'Isn't that a little like spying?'

She saw the rueful comprehension in his eyes, then he grunted, '*Ugh!*' and clutched at his chest, doubling over a little as though hurt.

For a moment she was nonplussed, until he looked up with a wicked grin, and she realised with an incredulous bubble of laughter that he was fooling.

He straightened up and left her with the smile still on his mouth, and her laughter followed him.

She hadn't thought him capable of such lighthearted fun, and the surprise lingered as a kind of quiet joy, long after he left. She felt happier than she had in months.

Of course it was too good to last. But it did carry her through the darkness to the winter's end, while the blizzard winds hurled the blown snow against their frail shelters until the buildings were all but buried, and the outside temperatures fell so low that the cold itself became a savage, inimical power against the human creatures who dared to challenge the raw forces of nature that surrounded them so overwhelmingly.

Dain sought her company no more often than before, but it did seem to Kerin that his eyes held a new warmth when he looked at her, and his voice had lost its icy edge. And when at the end of July a blood-red band appeared and glowed on the horizon, herald of the returning sun, and she sought his eyes with a smile on her lips, his answering smile had none of the sardonic quality she had used to see in it.

After the first excitement, the gradual return of the Antarctic daylight was met with a kind of sleepy, blinking wonder. The base inhabitants were like hibernating animals coming slowly to life with the advent of the spring. By the end of August they were getting four hours of light a day, although the temperature remained a chilling minus fifty degrees.

Kerin noted in her neat handwriting that some of the men had become absentminded and forgetful, but the irritability of early winter was less common. And when the rising sun had been greeted formally with celebration and the raising of the flags she recorded for Professor Prince the sudden increase in complaints of headache among the men. They blamed it on the unaccustomed sunlight, but she wondered if the psychologist would agree. One thing she was relieved about was that Eddie seemed quite his old self, excepting headaches of his own.

On the first day of September the first Hercules flew into McMurdo Sound from New Zealand, and later Hillary welcomed a cargo of mail, culinary delicacies and fresh spring flowers.

The cook turned the avocados, fresh milk and fruit, yoghurt and the rest into a feast, and Kerin arranged the flowers in the mess, amused to find now and then a man sitting and contemplating them almost with awe, as though they had nearly forgotten that such miracles existed.

She took her mail to her own room to read, opening a bulky envelope to find a long, scrawling and rambling letter from her friend and flatmate telling her the girl who had taken her place and got engaged and planned to move out soon, and that Cara would keep it for her return if she liked.

That was a stroke of luck, and she would accept the offer. All the other news seemed remote and unreal, even the paragraph in which Cara said that Roger was impatient for her return. She had seen him recently, it seemed, and gone out to dinner with him. It was not the first time Cara had mentioned him. Her first two letters had hinted that he missed Kerin dreadfully, and there was an undertone of reproach, but as Kerin refused to discuss him in her replies Cara had ceased mentioning his name.

There was a bank statement, a redirected letter from an old school friend who wrote about once a year and hadn't known about Kerin's Antarctic venture, and a long affectionate letter from her mother, in which Kerin caught a faint undertone of wishful thinking that she would settle down and stop gallivanting off literally to the ends of the earth.

The letter from Roger she left until last. It was, rather surprisingly, thinner than either Cara's or her mother's, and somehow less satisfying as well. He mentioned the dinner he had had with Cara—— '... a very pleasant evening. She's a good friend to you and a very sweet girl ...' Kerin smiled faintly at that. Not that it wasn't true, but she had thought Roger rather patronised Cara's naïve frankness, preferring a more sophisticated manner. He wrote about the magazine and about people they both knew, and ended with his love. And she wasn't sure if the dissatisfaction she felt was something that came through in his letter or was something in herself.

As the spring progressed, Dain's manner seemed to undergo another change. Not only with Kerin but with the men, he became harder and more exacting. The base had to be dug out of the snow and all the the equipment checked over, repaired where necessary and made ready for the new team which would arrive in October.

Exasperated with the implacable note in his voice as he spoke to one of the men about some work he had done on one of the machines, Kerin dared to remonstrate with him.

'Did you have to be so hard on him?' she asked. 'Anyone can make a mistake, and you know what a strain the winter's been on everyone.'

There was no softening in the harsh expression as he turned to look at her, and his voice was cool and hard. 'Sure I know. I also know what I'm doing.'

He had begun to swing away from her, and in irritated pique, she said, 'In other words, mind my own business?'

He swung back to look at her. 'That's right,' he said tightly. 'Do that. Maybe you'll learn a thing or two.'

He strode away across the deep snow, and Kerin stood shivering in a sudden blast of cold wind. *The chill factor*, she thought, *that's the important thing*. The Antarctic was beautiful and when there was no wind, spring and summer days could be warmly benign. It was the sudden icy winds that froze the blood.

But in the next week or so she began to perceive dimly what he had meant. Her observations of the men began to show a peculiar lethargy and incompetence, a 'don't care' attitude to their work that was quite out of keeping with the high calibre of the chosen men who made up the base staff. And she began to see that Dain's apparent tightening of discipline was necessary. Sloppiness didn't pay in this climate, and the base must be in good order for the new staff.

She also saw that some of the men disproportionately resented their commander's insistence on efficiency, and found that it bothered her. She mentioned her observations to Dain, one day, and warned him that some of the staff were beginning to express dislike for him.

'Should I be bothered?' he asked her sardonically.

'Aren't you? We've been through the winter together, it's some sort of bond. Surely you don't want them to hate you.'

'It's the season for it,' he said laconically, and turned away.

Kerin had begun to feel some sort of alliance with him, when she realised that he had recognised a psychological pattern in the men's strange unwillingness to work. But this cool self-sufficiency chilled her. No wonder he had been chosen as leader! He needed no one, had no dependence on the good opinion of other people.

It was a relief when Mitch and Guy suggested a dog-sled journey across the ice shelf to break the monotony. It was good to be pulled over the snow again, the dogs' breath smoking in the air and the cold pale sky arching over the white, blue-shadowed snow. The sea-ice was a milky green sheet and seals basked lazily by the breathing holes they had chewed in it near the ice-whitened water.

They were on their way back when disaster struck. The dogs were suddenly shoulder-deep, and Mitch called them to a halt. The firm ice had begun to melt already, and the way looked dangerous. They turned, and Guy took an ice axe and probed carefully for a safe direction. His boots sank ominously on loose, mushy ice that only an hour ago had been firm and hard as thick glass. The ice axe went through the thin footing to the water beneath, and it looked as though they were on a small, melting island.

Guy called, 'I think it's safe here!'

'Hold on to the lead harness,' Mitch told him, and they edged forward gently, but suddenly Guy's left leg sank without warning, and as he struggled to regain his balance, the dogs overran him as he sank further and there was a nightmare few minutes when he disappeared and the dogs milled and pulled until Mitch's shouted commands brought them out of the melt, dragging a sodden Guy with them.

Kerin's heart was beating fast, but there was no time to be afraid. Guy must be kept as warm as was possible in the circumstances, and while Mitch sorted out the now thoroughly tangled traces, she helped a shivering young field assistant into spare clothing kept on the sled.

'We'll go for broke!' Mitch said grimly, and with Guy back on the sledge he headed the dogs at breakneck speed across a dog-leg course that had them wallowing at a couple of points but finally brought them in to a firmer footing.

Guy got off and began to run beside the sledge in an effort to keep warm, but suddenly dropped face down on the ice.

With an effort Kerin and Mitch lifted him back on, where he came round and began insisting there was nothing wrong with him.

'Only hypothermia, mate,' Mitch muttered grimly, knowing that his diagnosis was confined by the patient's illogical belief that nothing was the matter.

Kerin was vastly relieved when they got Guy back to the base and Dain took over.

As soon as they had got him warmed and into bed to recover from the effects of freezing and exposure, Mitch reassured her, Guy would be just fine. But she wasn't fully certain of that until Dain himself assured them the patient was very little the worse for his experience.

'All the same,' he said, 'I've told him to stay in bed for the next forty-eight hours. And,' he added to the waiting group of men who had gathered in the mess to hear Kerin and Mitch tell them what had happened, 'I don't want anyone smuggling alcohol in to him. That's one thing he doesn't need.'

Later, Kerin and Mitch were allowed to visit Guy in his room. 'Hey, you two,' he said, 'thanks a lot—I mean that.'

'Nothing to thank us for,' Mitch disclaimed gruffly, and Kerin agreed.

'Well, thanks anyway!' said Guy, holding out his hand to clasp Nat Mitchell's, and then taking Kerin's hand in his, looking up at her with a meaning glint in his eyes. 'I want to thank you properly, Kerin,' he said, tugging her down towards him. But she turned her cheek as he made to kiss her lips, and straightened up, laughingly saying, 'I can see you're on the mend, my lad!'

He had a book on his knee and a pencil in his hand, and she asked, turning the subject, 'What are you doing?'

Guy grimaced. 'Crossword puzzles. I used to be keen on them when I was at school, but I'm finding this one a bit much for me. Guess I haven't enough vocabulary.'

'Would a thesaurus help?' she asked. 'I've got one if you'd like to borrow it?'

Guy looked interested. 'That would be beaut, Kerin! If I have to stay here I've got to have something to do, and I can tell you it gets damned disheartening never getting one of these out. A dictionary isn't really much use.'

'I'll get it now,' she offered, and left him with Mitch.

She had to rummage for the book, because she hadn't actually used it since coming here, but it was an occasional tool which it was frustrating to be without when she couldn't quite come up with the right word for something in what she was writing. She knew that crossword enthusiasts as well as writers found Roget's lists of similar and opposite words invaluable.

She went back to Guy's room to find that Mitch had left.

'Sorry to be so long,' she said. 'I had some trouble finding it.'

'That's okay.' He had put down his pencil and looked rather pale.

'Feeling groggy?' she asked him sympathetically.

'A bit tired,' he confessed. 'Like to tuck me up?' he grinned wanly.

Kerin smiled back and took the book of crosswords off the bed to put on the table. Guy watched her movements and as she glanced back at him, she thought that he looked very young. She straightened the cover over him, and he moved his hand to take her left one, looking at the ring on her third finger. 'Is this genuine?' he asked. 'I mean, are you really engaged?'

'Of course,' she said.

She tugged gently, but he held her hand, his fingers light but strong. 'Some of us wondered,' he said. 'We thought maybe it was just to make sure no one got out of line—you being the only woman.'

'Why should you think that?'

He leaned back on the pillows to survey her impudently. 'The general opinion seemed to be that if any of *us* had managed to put a ring on your finger we wouldn't be hanging about back in New Zealand waiting for you to come home. What sort of a guy is he?'

'An understanding sort of guy,' she said steadily. 'And tall, dark and handsome for good measure. Now let go of me and go to sleep.'

Instead he tightened his grip, bringing her a little closer to the bed. 'Understanding, is he? Then would he mind if you kissed me goodnight?'

'*I'd* mind!' she said firmly, making an effort to disengage herself.

'Please, Kerin,' he wheedled softly. 'I might have died out there, you know.'

'You didn't,' she said practically, but he did look pale and young, and pleading, and even as his fingers loosened on her wrist she weakened a little and bent to give him a fleeting peck.

Obviously he was not as exhausted as he looked. His other hand moved with astonishing swiftness to hold the back of her head and for a few moments he kept her lips pressed firmly to his, releasing her with a small, triumphant laugh, saying, 'Thanks, Kerin. That was better than any tonic.'

She tried to look affronted, but his combination of effrontery and boyish pleading could be very disarming. She said, 'Goodnight, Guy,' and turned with a smile on her lips for the door, only to be brought up short by the sight of Dain blocking her way, his hand on the jamb as though he had been standing in the open doorway for some time.

He moved a little, but not enough to let her pass, and looking past her, asked Guy how he felt.

The young man looked smug as he said, 'Fine. I was just going to sleep.'

'We won't keep you, then,' said Dain. And only then did he allow Kerin to precede him from the room, taking her arm as he shut the door behind them. 'I want to see you,' he said. 'In my office.'

Once there, he closed that door, too, and she tried to fight down a feeling of being trapped.

'Do you make a habit of that?' he asked, indicating a chair which she ignored. Irritably he gave her a little push and said, 'Sit down and answer the question!' He himself leaned against the edge of the desk.

'A habit of what?' she countered.

'Kissing that young idiot!'

'Is that your business?' she asked, angry at the inquisitorial tone.

'*Yes.*' His answer was uncompromising. 'He's about the least stable personality on the base, and he has a drinking problem. I knew from the first that he had a yen for you, but I was stupid enough to think you'd have the sense not to encourage it. I should have known no woman could resist playing up to the flattery of having a good-looking young fool at her feet. For heaven's sake, couldn't you see he had enough problems without that!'

'Your prejudice is showing again!' she told him. 'I've never played up to flattery of any sort, and who I kiss is my own business.'

She could have explained, but she doubted he would understand, and in any case she was too angry to even think that he deserved any explanation.

Dain snapped fiercely, '*And mine!*'

She looked into his blazing eyes and had a sudden conviction that his anger had a more personal basis than concern for the welfare of the base staff and for Guy's equilibrium in particular. A small spark of triumph lit her own eyes, because for the first time she felt she held the upper hand. Softly she said, 'Why? Because you feel you're the only one entitled to kiss me?'

His eyes narrowed. 'Are you implying that I'm jealous?'

'Yes,' she said, smiling as she rose to her feet. 'I'm sorry, Commander—I forgot the basic rule, didn't I? Pat one, pat them all.'

She leaned over the small space between them and fleetingly brushed her lips against his, then turned to the door.

He moved so fast she had it open only a fraction before his hand came flat against it, almost directly in front of her face, and slammed it shut.

Instinctively she drew back, finding herself up against a hard chest. Then his hands dug into the soft skin of her upper arms and he turned her to face him, against her futile resistance.

'There's another rule,' he said, 'that you'd better learn. Don't tease the animals.'

His hand shifted to haul her cruelly close to him, and his mouth came down with uncompromising hardness on hers. It was less a kiss than an assault, a determined beating down of all barriers, a brutal invasion by an enemy, not a lover. Her struggles were ruthlessly contained by hands that didn't care if they hurt, and her lips forced apart with utter disregard for their softness. She made an effort to bite at him, and his hand tangled into her hair and ruthlessly tugged back her head so that she gave a soundless cry of pain that opened her mouth further under his and let him deepen his invasive exploration of it. She felt the heat and sensual arousal of his body through their clothes, and stiffened against it, but Dain didn't care. He was asking for nothing, not even trying to arouse a response from her, but only taking what his strength could wrest from her.

She wondered in panic if he was ever going to stop, and when at last he did, dropping his hands from her, she groped behind her to lay her hands flat against the door, afraid that if she didn't lean on something she would fall, because the world seemed to sway about her dizzily.

She looked up, scarcely seeing the dark colour in his face, the glitter of his eyes, her own face pale and her eyes dark with emotion.

Bravely, she said, 'Thanks for the lesson, Commander. I won't forget it, I assure you. I wouldn't like to be mauled like that again!'

Her shaking hand found the door handle and she somehow kept her head erect until she had got herself into the passageway and away from him. Not until she reached the safety of her own room did she let the threatening tears have their way.

Guy recovered rapidly, complaining bitterly of Dain's ban on alcohol during his stay in bed, and making a beeline for the bar as soon as he was allowed up, drinking freely as he eyed Eddie's nude painting.

Having imbibed a little too much, he became maudlin and aggressive by turns, and Kerin, gently disengaging herself from his encircling arm as he reiterated his gratitude to her and Mitch, suggested he should return to bed.

'Come with me, then,' he leered.

'No, thanks,' she said shortly, glancing up to see Dain entering the room, his eyes unerringly finding her, going sharply from her to Guy.

Following her gaze, Guy said nastily, 'Oh, the commander wouldn't like it, would he? Objects to anyone having a bit of fun, doesn't he?'

'Don't be silly, Guy,' she said crossly.

'Didn't like you kissing me goodnight,' the man said sulkily. 'Could see it in his face. Jealous.'

Suddenly too angry to be tactful, Kerin snapped, 'Don't be stupid, Guy! You're drunk and making yourself ridiculous. For heaven's sake grow up and try to act like a man instead of a spoilt child!'

He blinked and flushed as she turned away with a curt goodnight and made for her own room, brushing by Dain without looking at him. She felt fed up, with the base, the season, the men, the whole set-up. For the first time she was sure she couldn't wait to leave the ice and get back to the normal world where there was green grass and trees and water that flowed and didn't have to be melted from blocks of ice. And where emotions could be controlled easily and didn't overwhelm as they did here.

She set herself to sorting out and packing some papers. Soon the next summer team would be here and she would be on her way back home. Her work here was nearly over.

She was putting folders into a cardboard carton, the floor strewn with piles of neatly typewritten sheets of paper, when the door was flung open without ceremony, and she straightened suddenly as Dain came into the room.

In his hand he held a small sheaf of similar papers, the small half-page sized sheets that she kept for magazine copy.

In clipped tones, he said, 'Yours, I believe.'

He held them out to her, and she took them, puzzled. Then her heart seemed to contract as she recognised the title on the first page: *Dain Ransome's Love*. This was the carbon copy, on thin paper, and she couldn't imagine how he had got hold of it. To the best of her knowledge she had packed both copies with the other stuff on her small desk in the flat, and left them stored in New Zealand.

Dain was speaking again, with held-in anger in his voice. 'You should have stayed for the performance,' he said, and she raised her head to look at him, not understanding. 'Did you get cold feet?' he asked. 'Or were you hoping I wouldn't recognise the author? You're not going to deny that it's yours?'

'No.' As she groped for something more to say, he went on.

'I must say Guy did it full justice, drunk or not. He

had the men splitting their sides. I believe you've both been hiding your talents. He's quite a ham, and you're a brilliant satirist. Unfortunately I find my sense of humour a little lacking where you're concerned. I managed to conceal the fact from the men—if you aimed at public humiliation I'm afraid your clever plan misfired a little. They're convinced that I'm a good sport and your little joke was all in good fun. But I don't need to pretend to you. It was a brilliant revenge—you found my most vulnerable spot and went for it quite ruthlessly. I didn't realise quite how thoroughly I'd exposed it to you. That'll teach me to talk to a journalist—or a psychologist! The combination—and your undoubted feminine charms—is a deadly one.'

Kerin was still trying to sort her scattered thoughts when he turned abruptly on his heel and left her. She tried to call him back, assure him she hadn't done what he thought, she could explain—but her throat closed up and her husky cry didn't reach him.

Almost dazed, she looked at the papers in her hand, riffling through them to check that her work had not been changed. *Satire*, he had called it, bitterly. But it hadn't been satire at all.

But Guy had apparently read it aloud to the men, and she could dimly see that read in a certain way—as Guy undoubtedly would read it, deliberately overplayed, sneering —it could be taken as satire, a rather cruel and cutting one at that, too close to truth not to hurt.

A white-hot anger filled her at the thought of Guy's doing that to her work without her permission. It must have somehow got slipped between the leaves of the thesaurus she had lent him, and he must have known that it was hers. His illogical resentment of Dain had warped his judgment and his ethics, and he had probably kept it, awaiting an opportunity to use it. And she hadn't helped, she realised, by letting fly at him tonight. He had been attempting to punish her as well as Dain.

Deliberately she tore the copy in half and dropped the

pieces in her overflowing wastebasket. Damn Guy, and damn Dain Ransome! He hadn't even asked for an explanation, but condemned her without a hearing. It was his way, and she was heartily sick of it. She looked at the ring on her third finger and thought of Roger with a sudden passion of nostalgia. She couldn't wait to be welcomed back into the haven of his arms and his calm, ordered, sophisticated life.

CHAPTER THIRTEEN

IT was ironic, Kerin thought afterwards, that while she was thinking this, Roger must have been trying to imagine how he was going to break their engagement.

Coming back was like entering a different world of sound and colour and people, so that her eyes and ears ached with it. By contrast the flat was quiet and Cara's greeting subdued, although her hug was more than merely affectionate.

She insisted on hearing all about the Antarctic, but her attention seemed to stray quite often, and then in the middle of a sentence she suddenly said, 'Roger's coming round later.'

'Is he?' said Kerin. 'But I didn't tell him I was home.'

'No, I know.' And Cara blushed painfully. 'Actually, he was coming, anyway.'

'I see.' She didn't, quite, but she began to when Roger appeared at the door, looking astounded to see her, and glancing meaningfully over her head at Cara before bending to kiss her cheek with an awkward air. Roger was never awkward, and as she returned his kiss Kerin experienced an oddly hollow feeling in her stomach.

Cara tactfully disappeared a few minutes later, and Kerin and Roger sat in silence, then both began to speak at once, laughed and stopped.

He said almost formally, 'My dear, I'm glad you're back.'

And she said, 'Yes. I expect you both are, you and Cara.'

He cast her a look that was surprised and almost appealing, and said stiffly, 'Cara's your best friend, isn't she?'

'Yes, a very good friend, as you said in one of your letters. Is that why she wouldn't let you break our engagement until I came home?'

Roger was startled and relieved. 'Did she—say something to you?'

'No. But she isn't good at pretending. She said before I went that I didn't deserve you, Roger. And she was right.'

The look of tenderness that entered his eyes then was not for her, and she said, 'You'd like your ring back, wouldn't you?'

'Kerin—I feel a heel about this——'

'No, don't!' she told him. 'It was much better to tell me than to be stupidly noble and try to pretend nothing has changed. I'm—I'm grateful, and glad for you and Cara.'

'You're being very generous.'

'No, not really. I realise now, if I'd loved you, Roger, I would have been prepared to marry you instead of going off to the Antarctic. And I think perhaps your feelings for me owed more to proximity than anything else.'

'Anything else?' he raised his brows and looked at her teasingly with a return of his natural suavity. 'My dear Kerin, have you looked in a mirror in the last five years?'

Kerin laughed. 'Keep your compliments for Cara—she's a lot more deserving of them than I am. Now, I'm going to have a long hot bath—a luxury I've been looking forward to for a whole year—and I suggest you take Cara out to some smashing place and tell her how you feel about her without any guilt feelings to interfere!'

She didn't move into the flat permanently after all, but found another place of her own, and also a new job. She attended their wedding about a month later and returned to the new flat feeling oddly deflated. She had not been in love with Roger and her heart wasn't broken, but life was suddenly very empty.

She had decided to redecorate her new home, and was in the middle of it one night in old jeans and a skimpy tee-shirt, her hair pulled into a ponytail and newspapers all over the floor in preparation for painting, when her door-bell rang.

Mentally cursing, and wondering who on earth it could

be, she picked her way to the door and opened it, to stand in stunned confusion as Dain surveyed her with a faint smile and said, 'Hello, Kerin. May I come in?'

She stood back and shut the door behind him before she trusted herself to speak. 'I'm sorry about the mess,' she said. 'I'm painting.'

'So I see.'

He was wearing a fitting open-necked shirt and dark trousers and his hair had been cut so that it just missed brushing the collar. And she couldn't stop staring at him.

He was staring back, and she put up a hand to tuck back a strand of hair, and said, 'I'm a bit of a mess, too.' She wasn't fishing for a compliment, just nervous.

But he didn't contradict her, and she led the way to the chairs drawn up in front of the empty grate and said, 'Sit down.' And then, 'Is this a social call?'

'I thought you'd like to know about Eddie,' he said. 'He went into hospital for tests when he got back, and they found what they called some minimal neurological disturbance, but he's going to be fine.'

'I'm very glad,' Kerin said. She stood up. 'Would you like a cup of tea—a drink?'

'No, thanks.'

She sat down again, perched on the edge of the chair, and clasped her restless hands together.

Dain looked at her fingers and asked, 'Where's Roger's ring?'

'I—wouldn't wear it for painting,' she said.

Then he asked softly, 'Where's Roger?'

And Kerin blurted out, 'Married to my best friend!'

She hadn't meant to say it, but it suddenly seemed pointless to pretend. What did it matter if he knew? He wouldn't care, one way or the other.

But when he suddenly exploded into laughter, she stood up and cut off the sound with a stinging blow to his lean cheek.

Before she could move back Dain had grabbed her wrist and she found herself pulled down on to his knee. Then he kissed her, her furious struggling of no avail against his easy strength.

She wrenched her mouth away from the hard pressure of his to gasp, 'Stop it!'

His answer was to pull the ribbon that held her hair until it came off, and he could tangle his fingers into the soft tresses it released and make her turn back to him.

She strained against him, saying breathlessly, 'You *beast*!'

But she said it against his mouth, a mouth that choked the words off and devastated her lips, demanding her unwilling submission. She freed one of her hands from his brutal embrace and pushed against his chest, then clawed at the hand that held her hair, scoring his wrist.

He raised his head to catch at her wrist and hold it in a cruel grasp. 'Cat!' he muttered.

'Swine!' Kerin retaliated with heat.

Dain laughed again, and anger renewed her struggles, making him more determined than ever to hold her, and his hands became hard as iron. Tersely, he said, 'Don't fight me, Kerin. You'll get hurt.'

'I'm *already* hurt!' she panted, but she had to stop because it was useless, and although he still held her he had gone strangely still.

'Why?' he demanded in an odd voice. 'Because I laughed?'

Kerin looked away, her body stiff in his hard embrace, her mouth tight.

Unexpectedly, he said, 'I'm sorry, it was tactless of me. I was just so damned glad.'

Involuntarily she turned to look at him. 'Glad?' she repeated blankly. Then, her face hardening defiantly, she said, 'If you think Roger jilted me, you're mistaken. The engagement was ended by mutual consent.'

Dain frowned. 'I'm not scoring points,' he said shortly. 'I tracked you down and came here to see you precisely to stop you marrying Roger.'

His hands had loosened a little, and when she moved

experimentally, he dropped her wrist and slid his hand on to the narrow band of warm skin that showed where her skimpy tee-shirt had ridden up. She grasped his wrist, but couldn't stop his hand moving up to caress the softness of a rounded breast. His eyes gleamed into hers and he said, 'You don't give a damn who marries Roger, do you?'

Waves of sensation washed over her body, and her feeble efforts to move his probing hand had no effect. Almost imperceptibly she shook her head, and saw his faint grin of response before he dipped his head and explored her neck with almost greedy pleasure, his mouth moving against her skin. She heard him murmur, 'I knew it,' as his fingers found her body's involuntary response to his lovemaking.

But she wasn't entirely lost to reason yet. She twisted suddenly out of his arms and stood up, backing off from him as he followed suit, until he stopped in front of her.

'What do you want from me?' she asked, trying to breathe steadily, to keep her voice even.

His brows raised, he grinned faintly, his eyes moving intimately over her body and then back to her face. 'I thought I'd made that obvious. But if you want it in words . . .'

'*No!* But you can have the answer in words—or one word. And it's no.'

His face went quite blank for a moment, and Kerin felt a painful jab of mingled hurt and gladness. He wanted her, and he had thought he could take her from Roger and make her his—for just as long as he continued to want her. In between seasons in the Antarctic and lecture tours overseas, of course. Or even, perhaps, just for tonight. He wasn't a marrying man, he had no use for permanent relationships, but he had enjoyed making love to her, kissing her, a few times. Perhaps he knew what she had finally admitted to herself, that she was in love with him. But even that wouldn't make her give up her self-respect in a fleeting love affair that could lead to nothing.

'Tell me why,' he insisted.

'Does there have to be a reason?'

'Yes. And don't bring Roger into it. You've never acted as though he really mattered to you—and you just admitted you don't care about him.'

'If that's a good enough reason,' she retorted, 'then it applies equally to you.'

'You care,' he said quietly. 'I've seen it in your eyes a dozen times. And I've felt it when I've kissed you—even when you fought me. Just as I felt it in myself as I fought you.'

Coldly she said, 'You're talking about a physical reaction. You're not the only man who can make me feel like that.'

Sudden anger tautened his jaw. 'I'm talking about a good deal more than physical reactions. That's only a part of what we've shared, Kerin, and you know it. We understand each other on a much deeper level than mere sex. That's why our kisses have been so good—when you've let them be. Because they express more than surface attraction— there's an awareness between us that starts in our minds, and don't pretend you don't know what I mean. That piece on my relationship with Antarctica may have been written to punish me, but you're the only person in the world who knows me well enough to plan that particular form of hurt.'

She said quickly, 'I scarcely knew you when I wrote it. I did it before I left for the Antarctic—after the first time we met. Not for publication, though. And I didn't mean Guy to see it. He must have found it in a book I lent him. I didn't know it was there. I'm sorry for what happened— and sorry he made it sound like satire. It wasn't meant to be.'

Slowly he said, 'Then you weren't hitting back for the way I reacted to your kissing Guy?'

Kerin looked at him with faint challenge. 'To my kissing Guy?'

A faint colour appeared along his cheekbones. 'All right. To your accusation of jealousy. You were right, and I wouldn't admit it to myself. So I took it out on you—a last-ditch stand against defeat.'

'Defeat?'

Dain moved to lean a shoulder against the mantel and said with sardonic self-mockery, 'Capitulation—surrender. I fought it from the first time I met you. I saw your face a couple of times when I was lecturing that day, and found myself talking to you, because I knew you understood. Even then I scented danger, and made the excuse that you were a scheming woman, to keep myself from trying to bring you into my life. When you turned up on the base, I knew I had to get rid of you for my peace of mind. I thought of every excuse I could—dredged up reasons out of the past, told myself they were valid. There had been women who made trouble among the men in the Antarctic, and I convinced myself you inevitably must be one of them. You were too beautiful not to.'

'But you let me come back, when I went to the Pole. You could have . . .'

'Yes, I could have made sure you didn't return. But you challenged me, remember. And I decided that I wouldn't use underhand methods, I would fight the battle out in the open.'

'I take it we're talking about the famous battle of the sexes,' Kerin said wryly. 'Is it any use telling you I wasn't a contender?'

'I know,' he admitted. 'You're a fighter, though. You came through with flying colours, without any help from me.'

'You didn't help,' she said. 'You were suspicious and very quick to jump to conclusions.'

'Yes,' Dain admitted. 'When I looked at you I couldn't see straight. I was totally convinced that everyone must want you as much as I did, and you would add to everyone's frustrations, and you proved me wrong by being a tactful safety valve instead. And when I tried to protect you, you pointed out that you had the same obligations and rights as everyone else. I wouldn't have stopped any of the men from diving—the thought of *you* down there, drowning or freezing, terrified me.'

Remembered anger sparkled in Kerin's eyes. 'So it *was* because I was a woman!'

'Because you were the woman I was in love with,' Dain corrected. 'Although I was still trying not to admit it, then. I tried until I got back to New Zealand—told myself it was temporary madness. But it wasn't. And I'm not fighting any more. You're brave and beautiful and tough, and you've won a victory you didn't seek. Well, I suppose there's some poetic justice in it. The one woman who's made a havoc of my emotions and a desert of everything I've lived for turns me down.'

His mouth still looked derisive, and his face wore its man of ice look. The words that he was saying didn't go with his controlled manner.

Kerin protested, 'You can't mean that! I don't mean as much to you as that. More than Antarctica.'

Dain looked at her and straightened. 'More than my cold mistress? I'd give her up tomorrow if you would be my wife.' Unbelievably, his voice shook.

'*Wife?*' She searched his face, trying to see behind the icy mask he had assumed. 'You said nothing about marriage,' she reminded him.

'What?' Suddenly life flowed into his face, the cool eyes blazed. 'My God, what did you think I was saying? I told you it was my intention to stop you marrying Roger, that I loved you—you said you didn't need the words.'

'I find that I do,' she said, her voice more composed than she would have thought possible.

He reached for her then, his hands hard on her shoulders, dragging her to him. 'I'm asking you to *marry* me!' he said almost savagely.

A tiny laugh rose in her throat. 'That's a very rough proposal,' she complained.

'Don't tease me, Kerin, damn you!' He gave her a small shake, but the tiny thump her heart gave was caused by the uncertainty in his eyes as he waited for her answer. 'Yes or no?' he demanded.

'I somehow don't think you'd take no for an answer,' she

said shakily. His hands moved to cup her head, his fingers hard, but she could feel them trembling. 'Yes,' she whispered, and saw the doubt leave his eyes before his mouth claimed hers and the man of ice, disappeared, melting in the heat of passion that had her clinging to him dizzily until he lifted his head and took her with him back to the chair.

His hand caressed her back beneath the shirt, and with her lips against his cheek she murmured, 'I won't stand for being left behind while you spend seasons on the ice, you know.'

'I told you——'

Kerin put her fingers against his mouth. 'I want to come with you,' she said, and felt his body stiffen and relax, his smiling eyes searching hers. 'I mean it,' she assured him. 'I'm hooked, too. You know those historic huts?' He nodded, and she went on, 'They have caretakers, each summer, don't they?'

'Yes. What are you thinking of?'

'A sort of extended honeymoon. Would they take a married couple?'

Dain laughed softly. 'A crazy place for a honeymoon!'

'But beautiful.'

'Yes, beautiful. You're not going to be a jealous wife, are you?'

'Of your other love? I love it too. Professor Prince is curious to know if people born on the ice would adapt—like the Eskimos—over a period of time.' She looked up into his quizzical eyes and buried her face against the warmth of his shoulder, saying, 'Well, it's possible.'

'As long as you love me, anything is possible,' he said. He lifted her chin with his hand and read the assurance in her eyes, and said against her mouth as it moved sweetly to meet his kiss, 'Anything at all.'